Samuel French Acting Edition

The Mating Game

A Comedy

by Robin Hawdon

I0591847

ıⅡSAMUEL FRENCHⅡı

SAMUELFRENCH.COM   **SAMUELFRENCH.CO.UK**

FOR PRODUCTION ENQUIRIES

UNITED STATES AND CANADA
Info@SamuelFrench.com
1-866-598-8449

UNITED KINGDOM AND EUROPE
Plays@SamuelFrench.co.uk
020-7255-4302

Each title is subject to availability from Samuel French, depending upon
country of performance. Please be aware that THE MATING GAME may
not be licensed by Samuel French in your territory. Professional and
amateur producers should contact the nearest Samuel French office or
licensing partner to verify availability.

THE MATING GAME

(under the title AS LONG AS IT'S WARM)

was originally presented at the
New Theatre, Bromley,
on July 3, 1967

Cast

Draycott Harris	*Simon Brent*
Honey Tooks	*Betty McDowall*
James Harris	*Ray Cooney*
Julia Carrington	*Veronica Strong*
Mrs. Finney	*Hazel Coppen*

Directed by David Paulson

❧ ❧

THE MATING GAME

was presented by John Gale and Ray Cooney at the
Apollo Theatre, London,
opening June 14, 1972

Cast

Draycott Harris	Clive Francis
Honey Tooks	Aimi MacDonald
James Harris	Terry Scott
Julia Carrington	Julia Lockwood
Mrs. Finney	Avril Angers

Directed by Ray Cooney

SETTING

The action of the play takes place in Draycott's penthouse bachelor flat, somewhere in Park Lane, London.

The time is the present.

ACT I

Scene 1
The early hours of the morning.

Scene 2
Later the same morning.

ACT II

Scene 1
The same evening.

Scene 2
The next morning.

Note: The set need not be as elaborate as that which was used in London. The television dropping in from the ceiling can be dispensed with; the bedroom/office furniture need not be on a "revolve" as indicated in the script, but can simply be pushed in and pulled out by stagehands. In fact, in London everything was manipulated by stagehands and "cued" from the prompt corner. The "electronic warfare" sequence in Act II, Scene 1 can be as simple or complicated as the production can manage. The most difficult part of the building of the set is the bed, but even this can be worked on the principle of the matchbox, although it is much funnier for it to go up into the wall rather than slide in and out.

ACT I

Scene 1

(Time: The Present. The scene is Draycott Harris's smart penthouse bachelor flat somewhere in Park Lane. The room is on two levels. The upper level is a step or two higher than the lower, about four feet deep, and runs around the perimeter of the room. There are four doors leading off the upper level; the front door is upstage R of center, and the kitchen door is immediately next to this on its L. In the wall D.L. is the bathroom door. In the wall U.R. is the door to the spare room, although this is concealed as part of a bookcase.

At curtain up the room is set as a bedroom with a large double bed upstage L of C., a wardrobe with mirror L. and a dressing table R. However, the flat also serves as Draycott's place of business and, at the press of a series of switches, the room is turned into an efficient modern office. Then the dressing table R. revolves and out comes a desk complete with typewriter, telephones etc. The wardrobe L. revolves and in its place is a filing cabinet (or alternatively these could be separate trucks which roll in and out). The bed swings up into the back wall and on the underside is a large blown-up black and white photograph of Draycott Harris in his TV studio.

There are two more pieces of equipment which can be used in either bedroom or office mode. One is a low cocktail cabinet concealed in the wall down R. which slides into the room at the press of a switch. The other is the TV. set which comes down at the press of a switch from the ceiling to a comfortable position six feet from the ground at the foot of the bed. There are three pieces of furniture on the lower level of the room which double for both office and bedroom: an armchair, a small settee and a coffee table.

Everything is ultra modern.
The panel which controls all the gadgets is set in the upstage wall
between the bed and the kitchen. On the wall to the R. of the front
door is an entry-phone which communicates with the main door
of the building, with a button to admit callers. In whichever wall
there is space is a window through which can be seen the tops of
the buildings in the Park Lane area.
When the curtain rises the stage is in total darkness. After a moment
there is the sound of a key in the lock, and the flat door opens
admitting a brief glimmer of light in which two figures are seen,
their arms round each other. The door closes and the sound of
rapturous passion is heard in the darkness.)

DRAKE. Ohhh!
HONEY. Mmmm!
DRAKE. What a night!
HONEY. What a terrific night!
DRAKE. You're stunning!
HONEY. You're beautiful!
DRAKE. I want you.
HONEY. Who's arguing?

(Together.)

DRAKE. Ohhhh!   HONEY. Mmmm!

(Slight pause.)

DRAKE. *(Alarmed.)* What's that?
HONEY. What?
DRAKE. On my cheek. A spider!
HONEY. Don't be silly — my false eyelash has come off.
DRAKE. Oh.
HONEY. Where's the bed then?
DRAKE. Over here.

(They collapse in an embrace onto the bed.)

(Together.)

    DRAKE. Ohhhh!   HONEY. Mmmm!

(Suddenly there is a shout and a figure erupts out of the bed between them.)

    JAMES. Hey!! Wossat?? Whoosat??

(They scream and break apart.)

    DRAKE. Who's that?
    JAMES. It's me — who's that?
    HONEY. The lights, the lights for God's sake!

(DRAKE switches on the lights and the pandemonium ceases. JAMES HARRIS is sitting up in the bed clutching the cover to him as if it's the only protection he has in the world.
JAMES is in his thirties, jovial and easy-going. DRAKE is in his twenties, better looking and more insecure than his brother. DRAKE is wearing a trendy jacket and shirt, JAMES appears to be wearing nothing. HONEY is a cool, wide-eyed blond who is wearing not a lot more — but it's very stylish.
The room is in its 'bedroom' state with the TV and cocktail cabinet concealed. James's clothes are flung on the armchair and his suitcase is to the R. of the flat door.)

    DRAKE. Good God — it's you!
    JAMES. Hello, old son.
    DRAKE. What the hell are you doing here?
    JAMES. Well that's a nice welcome.
    DRAKE. Sorry, but I ... I mean it's great to see you, but what ...?
    JAMES. I'm back.
    DRAKE. You're back?
    JAMES. I'm back.
    DRAKE. Well, you old bugger! *(They fling their arms round each other.)* I can't believe it! How long for?

JAMES. For good.

(They roar with laughter and clap each other on tile back.)

DRAKE. *(To HONEY.)* Can you believe it? He's back!

HONEY. I'm delighted! Who the hell is he?

DRAKE. Oh sorry, you two haven't met. Honey, meet my big brother, James.

JAMES. How d'you do — I won't stand up.

HONEY. How do you do.

DRAKE. *(To JAMES.)* Honey Tooks.

JAMES. Honey whats?

HONEY. Tooks!

JAMES. *(Shaking hands.)* Nice to meet you.

DRAKE. He's been in Australia.

JAMES. Three years.

DRAKE. *(Beaming at JAMES.)* And now you're back.

JAMES. I'm back.

HONEY. *(Dry.)* You picked a good moment.

DRAKE. *(Realizing.)* Ah.

JAMES. *(Realizing.)* Ah. Yes. You need the, er …. You want to, er …. Is there another bed?

DRAKE. No.

JAMES. Sorry to barge in, but the porter said it would be O.K. to make myself at home, so er ….

HONEY. You did.

(JAMES looks from DRAKE to HONEY.)

JAMES. I'll, er …. I'll go to a hotel.

DRAKE. It's one o'clock in the morning!

HONEY. Drake, darling, don't let's have a scene. I'll go.

DRAKE and JAMES. *(Together.)* No, you mustn't go!

HONEY. What else do you suggest? We all three share the bed?

JAMES. Well that's very …. *(Quickly.)* No, thank you. Look, Drake, old son, I'll get dressed, go out for a cup of coffee somewhere and come back later. *(To HONEY.)* How long do you think ….

(Quickly.) Say a couple of hours.

HONEY. *(Getting up. To DRAKE.)* It's been a great evening. We'll finish it off some other time.

DRAKE. *(Urgent.)* No, Honey, please!

JAMES. He was always the same. Couldn't wait for dessert.

DRAKE. Oh, shut up! *(To HONEY.)* He could sleep in the spare room.

JAMES. Thanks.

HONEY. It's no good, Drake. I can't concentrate with more than one man available.

JAMES. Who said I was available? *(Stands up in the bed, wrapping the bed-cover round himself.)* Look, I insist. I'm going.

HONEY. What as, Julius Caesar?

JAMES. Well, I'll change first.

(He waddles towards his clothes.)

HONEY. *(Stopping him.)* Don't bother, James, it's all settled. *(To DRAKE.)* Good-night, darling. Next time book the bed.

(She puts her arms round his neck and embraces him. JAMES stands there awkwardly.)

JAMES. Yes, well ... I'm glad we've sorted that out.... Hope I'm not in the way. What a nice room this is. *(They still don't break the embrace.)* Tell you what — I'll take a look at the spare room and see how I like it. Goodnight Miss er.... Whew! *(JAMES searches for the door, but can't find it as it's part of the bookcase. Tapping DRAKE's shoulder.)* Excuse me, I'm sorry to interrupt. But where is it?

(They break apart.)

DRAKE. Sorry. Behind you.

JAMES. Oh. *(JAMES leans on the bookcase and the door opens. He almost falls in.)* I've never slept in a bookcase.

(JAMES picks up his battered suitcase, goes in and shuts the door.)

DRAKE. *(Quickly.)* Look — you wait in the kitchen. I'll pack him off to bed with a quick cup of cocoa — then you can come back.

HONEY. It's two in the morning.

DRAKE. I'll have him there in five minutes.

HONEY. *(Dry.)* You do like your dessert, don't you?

DRAKE. Get in the kitchen.

JAMES. *(From the spare room.)* Not much room in here.

(DRAKE pushes HONEY into the kitchen and closes the door. As JAMES comes out of the spare room DRAKE quickly opens the front door and calls into the hall.)

DRAKE. 'Bye Honey! *(Turns innocently to JAMES.)* O.K.?

JAMES. Bit cramped with the ping pong table, the sauna *and* the rowing machine. I'd be better off on the settee, wouldn't I?

(He heads towards it. DRAKE catches him by the arm and steers him back.)

DRAKE. No, no. Much better in there. I snore.

JAMES. Oh. Well, I'm very sorry if I er… sabotaged your plans, old son.

DRAKE. That's O.K. It's great to see you.

JAMES. And you. God, have I had a hectic three years!

(JAMES heads for the sofa again. DRAKE stops him.)

DRAKE. I bet you have. Tell me about it in the morning.

JAMES. Morning?

DRAKE. It's very late.

JAMES. Yes, but I haven't seen you for three years. I could do with a drink.

DRAKE. Fine. How about a cup of cocoa.

JAMES. Cocoa?

DRAKE. You can take it to bed with you.

JAMES. I'd rather have something stronger. We need to celebrate.

DRAKE. *(Reluctantly.)* All right ... a quickie then.

JAMES. I tried to find some booze when I arrived. Where the hell do you keep it?

DRAKE. Voila!

(He presses a button and the cocktail cabinet slides in from the wall.)

JAMES. *(After a moment.)* Do the neighbors share that with you?

DRAKE. It's a penthouse flat. I don't have neighbors.

JAMES. My God, you've done well for yourself. When I left you'd just finished at university and were trying to break into acting. You'd got a one-room flat in Muswell Hill and a hundred pound overdraft.

DRAKE. Yep. Well now I've got a Park Lane apartment and a hundred thousand pound overdraft.

JAMES. That *is* success. How've you done it?

DRAKE. Television.

JAMES. Come again?

DRAKE. TV. The biggest influence on the planet.

(He presses a button and a large TV set comes down from the ceiling with its screen facing the bed. He presses again and it goes back.)

JAMES. You've made a fortune selling TV sets?

DRAKE. Where *were* you in Australia? Living in the bush?

JAMES. More or less.

DRAKE. I'm the biggest thing on the box. I'm on six nights a week.

JAMES. What are you, the weather forecast?

DRAKE. I've got a chat show. Famous personalities letting their hair down.

JAMES. It was Terry Wogan when I left.

DRAKE. Well it's me now. The Draycott Harris Show. This is me at work.

(Presses a button and the bed swings up into the wall almost taking JAMES with it. The underside shows the large blown-up photo of

Drake in the TV studio.)

JAMES. Good Lord! When mother wrote you were interviewing people I thought she meant on-street surveys like other out-of-work actors. So you're famous, are you?

DRAKE. I'm the biggest thing since Oprah Winfrey.

JAMES. *(Chuckles.)* I can't believe it. My little brother Draycott. Well, let's have that drink to celebrate.

DRAKE. *(Looking at his watch.)* A quick one then. What would you like? Champagne, Campari, Noilly Prat, Cinzano?

JAMES. I want a drink, not an after-shave. Got any beer?

DRAKE. *(Shaking his head.)* Don't drink it.

JAMES. Here, I've just remembered. I've got the very thing in my suitcase.

(He moves towards the study door.)

DRAKE. Don't you think we should get to bed?

JAMES. I want to hear about your rise to fame. If only Dad had lived to see you on the telly.

DRAKE. He never thought I'd make anything. He'd have died happy.

JAMES. I know what he'd have done if he'd seen you in that gear.

DRAKE. *What?*

JAMES. Died laughing.

(He goes into the spare room. The kitchen door immediately opens and HONEY appears.)

HONEY. Shall I serve breakfast?

DRAKE. We're just going to have one quick drink, I promise.

HONEY. Well if I'm waiting, so am I.

(She moves down to the bar.)

DRAKE. Please, Honey, stay in the kitchen.

HONEY. I keep better dipped in alcohol.
JAMES. *(Singing off.)* Waltzing Matilda — waltzing Matilda....

(JAMES comes out of the spare room with a bottle and DRAKE hurriedly presses a button. HONEY, who has been standing by the dressing table, disappears on the revolve and the office desk comes into view.)

JAMES. *(As he enters.)* Now, this stuff will put hairs....
HONEY. *(As she vanishes.)* Eeee!

(JAMES stops on hearing the noise and turns just as the desk settles into position.)

JAMES. What was that?
DRAKE. The cat.
JAMES. Is it stuck in the wall? *(Sees the desk.)* That wasn't there before, was it?
DRAKE. No. I er ... I was just demonstrating how the place is convertible from bedroom to office at the press of a button.

(He moves down to the cocktail cabinet and during the ensuing dialogue gets a corkscrew which he gives to JAMES to uncork the bottle.)

JAMES. If you're so filthy rich why can't you afford an office *and* a flat?
DRAKE. This way it's tax-deductible.
JAMES. Clever. And is Honey whatsername tax-deductible, too?
DRAKE. Yes actually. She's my P.R. girl.
JAMES. *(Chuckling.)* What's P.R. stand for — 'permanently rampant'?

(DRAKE quickly pulls him away from the revolve.)

DRAKE. Ssh! 'Public Relations.' She's starting work tomorrow.

JAMES. What was tonight — a rehearsal? So she gives you private relations by night and public relations by day, eh? Does she take dictation in bed too?

DRAKE. My secretary does that.

JAMES. You've got a secretary too?

DRAKE. Honey looks after my affairs at the studios....

JAMES. You have them there as *well*?

DRAKE. *(Ignoring this.)* ... and Julia organizes everything else. Contracts, fan mail, interviews....

JAMES. And is Julia as obliging as Honey?

DRAKE. Not remotely.

JAMES. That's just as well.

DRAKE. She's a very high-minded girl. *(He looks at his watch and has a surreptitious listen at where HONEY is secreted. JAMES has the cork out and is pouring the drink into glasses. DRAKE looks at it suspiciously.)* Tell me James, what is this stuff?

JAMES. Australian schnapps.

DRAKE. Australian *what?*

JAMES. It was presented to me by a sheep-farmer from the outback. I think he brewed it himself. Well here's to the Draycott Harris Show. Long may it run.

DRAKE. *(Uncertainly)* Cheers.

(DRAKE tries a sip)

JAMES. *(Watching him warily.)* What's it like?

DRAKE. *(Thoughtfully.)* Not too bad. Tastes a bit like ....

(The effect hits him like a bomb, and leaves him gasping for air.)

JAMES. Like what?

DRAKE. *(Hoarse.)* Rocket fuel.

JAMES. *(Looking at the label.)* I hope it won't melt your glasses.

DRAKE. (*Regaining his breath.)* Well I'm not dying alone — it's your turn.

(JAMES tries a cautious sip. After a few seconds the effect hits him.)

JAMES. Wow! It reaches parts you didn't know you had, doesn't it?

DRAKE. *(Sucking his teeth.)* My teeth have gone soft.

JAMES. *(Eventually.)* Well, it's got a funny way of traveling but it seems to know where to go. Probably best to get it down in one gulp.

DRAKE. Cheers.

JAMES. Cheers.

(They both drain their glasses and wait for the effect.)

DRAKE. Yuk!

JAMES. Yuk! *(Holds out the bottle.)* More?

DRAKE. Yes, please.

(JAMES fills their glasses.)

JAMES. Up the revolution.

(They drink and the ghastly effect hits again.)

HONEY. *(Off.)* Hey! I want a drink!

JAMES. *(To DRAKE, surprised.)* That was clever. Do you do funny voices on your show?

DRAKE. Yes. *(As JAMES fills his glass.)* This really ought to be the last one, Jim.

JAMES. You said you wanted a drink.

DRAKE. *(Loudly for HONEY's benefit.)* Well I'm anxious to get to bed.

JAMES. All right, I'm not deaf!

DRAKE. You see, I have to be up early to get to the studio. It's a long day. Discussions all morning on the format for the show, meet the guests in the afternoon, camera rehearsals, then the program goes out at 8 p.m.

JAMES. Six nights a week?

DRAKE. Six nights a week.

JAMES. I'm surprised you've got enough energy left for old

'permanently rampant.'

DRAKE. Ssh!

HONEY. *(Off.)* I'll give you 'Rampant'!

JAMES. *(To DRAKE.)* Are you going to practice all night? *(DRAKE smiles weakly as his glass is filled again.)* You really live it up, don't you. I hope this stuff doesn't ruin your potential. Cheers!

DRAKE. Cheers. *(They knock it back in one. The expected effect is less now.)* It grows on you, doesn't it?

JAMES. Maybe it's a hair restorer. *(Chuckles.)* Hey, you should have me on your show. I'm good at funny stories.

(He fills the glasses.)

DRAKE. But my show is a sophisticated show, Jim. Culture and current affairs.

JAMES. Fine. "There was a young man from Caerphilly...."

DRAKE. I don't think so.

(The front door opens behind them and MRS. FINNEY enters. She is middle-aged and lugubrious. She stands there eyeing DRAKE and JAMES.)

JAMES. No, I know a better one. "There was a young man from Madras —"

MRS. F. Good morning!

JAMES. *(Examining DRAKE's lips.)* How do you do that?

DRAKE. *(Turning.)* What are you doing here at this hour, Mrs. Finney?

JAMES. *(Turning.)* Oh.

MRS. F. Just checking. I saw your light on and wondered if my old man had done the right thing letting this one in. *(She gives JAMES a withering glance.)* He says he's your brother but you can never tell these days, can you?

DRAKE. *(To JAMES.)* Mrs. Finney — the porter's wife.

JAMES. Nice to meet you.

MRS. F. Can't say the same. Not at this hour.

DRAKE. She's also my housekeeper.

MRS. F. And it's not a good time to start making up beds.

JAMES. Ah, yes.... Sorry.

MRS. F. Where are you sleeping?

JAMES. *(Defensively.)* Never mind — I can look after myself.

MRS. F. *(Eyeing his attire.)* Doesn't look much like it.

DRAKE. The spare room, Mrs. Finney.

JAMES. If there's space in there.

MRS. F. I'll make up the ping pong table. Or does that outfit mean you'll be practicing yoga all night.

JAMES. It means I've got nothing on underneath.

MRS. F. I see.

JAMES. *(Pulling his cover tighter.)* No, you don't.

MRS. F. *(To DRAKE.)* And have you been working as well as playing charades?

DRAKE. Working? No.

MRS. F. Then why don't you keep your desk in the right place?

(She takes a pace to the control panel.)

DRAKE. No, don't!

(But she has already pressed the button. The desk revolves, and HONEY appears with the dressing table, glowering.)

MRS. F. Good God Almighty!

HONEY. No, just me.

JAMES. *(Incredulously.)* It's incredible. He keeps them in cold storage.

MRS. F. *(To HONEY.)* Are there any more where you came from?

HONEY. I don't know —it was dark in there. *(To DRAKE.)* I could have suffocated!

DRAKE. I'm sorry, Honey.

JAMES. Now I know what P.R. stands for. 'Push-Button Relief.'

HONEY. *(Derisive.)* Well that's better than 'Permanently Rampant.'

JAMES. *(Abashed.)* Sorry.

HONEY. It's been a fascinating evening, Draycott.

DRAKE. Honey, don't be cross.

HONEY. I'm not cross. I love playing on the roundabouts at one in the morning.

(She opens the front door.)

DRAKE. Hold on a minute. We were all just going to bed, weren't we, Mrs. Finney.

MRS. F. I should hope so.

HONEY. Then I hope the three of you will be very comfortable. Good night.

(She goes, closing the door.)

DRAKE. *(Despairing.)* Oh God!

JAMES. Hiding them in the furniture. You must be desperate.

MRS. F. You don't know the half of it. Get him within three feet of a woman and the only thing that isn't at attention is his shoelaces.

DRAKE. Thank you, Mrs. Finney.

MRS. F. *(Seeing the bottle.)* Celebrating are we?

DRAKE. Just a drop before bed.

MRS. F. That's what my husband says every night and he hasn't been to bed sober for twenty years. What is it?

JAMES. Australian Schnapps.

MRS. F. Never heard of it.

JAMES. *(Wickedly.)* Try some.

MRS. F. *(Pleased.)* Oh, well….

DRAKE. Just a small one, Jim.

JAMES. *(Filling a glass to the top.)* Of course. *(Hands it to her.)* To get the full flavor you knock it back in one.

MRS. F. Right — bottoms up. *(She knocks it back. DRAKE and JAMES watch expectantly.)* Mmm. Subtle. I'll see to your room. *(She walks unaffected to the spare room door. DRAKE and JAMES react to each other and then look back at her. MRS. FINNEY gets to the door, opens it, but then goes the wrong side of it and disappears be-*

hind, walking into the wall with a loud thump. Pause. She reappears.)
Australian, you say?

JAMES. Yes.

MRS. F. I don't think it's traveled very well.

(She exits unsteadily.)

JAMES. Well I'll say this for you — you've got an original work-force!

DRAKE. *(Pacing.)* Oh God, I'm such an idiot!

JAMES. What?

DRAKE. I really cocked things up with Honey.

JAMES. Well, yes — I *would* have pushed off if I'd known a bit of nookie meant that much to you.

DRAKE. I suppose I did get a bit carried away. *(Awkwardly.)* You see, Jim, I've ... well I've got a bit of a problem.

JAMES. You certainly have, old son. You should try tranquilizers.

DRAKE. You see, the thing is ....

JAMES. Hang on a sec. Can you press a button and get that set-tee over here?

DRAKE. No.

JAMES. Pity. I'll have to walk.

(JAMES walks to settee and sits.)

DRAKE. The thing is this.... *(Tails off.)*

JAMES. What?

DRAKE. Can I have some more rocket fuel first?

(JAMES fills their glasses. They drink.)

JAMES. *(Beginning to get quite drunk.)* You know, you could clear drains with this stuff.

DRAKE. The thing is this, Jim....

JAMES. What thing?

DRAKE. My problem.

JAMES. Haven't we sorted that out yet?

DRAKE. It's serious!

JAMES. What is it?

DRAKE. You promise not to laugh.

JAMES. Why, is it funny?

DRAKE. No, it isn't.

JAMES. Then why should I laugh?

DRAKE. Promise, damn you, promise!

JAMES. All right, if it's not funny I promise I won't laugh.

DRAKE. Look at me, Jim.

JAMES. *(Peering.)* I can see all three of you.

DRAKE. I've got all this. *(Indicates the room.)* Money. Fame. I mix with fascinating people. Beautiful women. I've got everything a man could want.

JAMES. You certainly have.

DRAKE. Except for one thing.

JAMES. What's that?

DRAKE. *(Hesitating)* I've never ....

JAMES. What?

DRAKE. I'm a ....

JAMES. What?

DRAKE. I've never ....

JAMES. WHAT?

DRAKE. Done it.

(Pause.)

JAMES. Done what?

DRAKE. *It.* I'm a virgin.

(Longer pause.)

JAMES. A what?

DRAKE. A virgin!

(Another pause.)

JAMES. What's that?

DRAKE. This is no time for gags!

JAMES. You?

DRAKE. Me. *(Further pause, then JAMES is convulsed with laughter.)* You promised!

JAMES. I'm sorry, I'm very sorry.... *(It takes JAMES several seconds to control himself.)* I'm not sure what I'm supposed to say.

DRAKE. Commiserate with me or something.

JAMES. That's very tragic.

DRAKE. I'm a freak!

JAMES. I'm not arguing. Tell me — is it by choice, circumstance or religion?

DRAKE. By fate.

JAMES. How do you mean, fate?

DRAKE. *(Pointing upwards.)* I mean that somebody up there's playing with me.

JAMES. On the roof?

DRAKE. Way up there. Whoever's in charge of sexual relations is having a damn good laugh at me.

JAMES. He's not the only one. What have you been doing all these years?

DRAKE. Trying!

JAMES. I see.

DRAKE. Every time it's about to happen something prevents it. You can't tell me it's not fate. I get the girl, it's all set to happen, and something else happens — bang!

JAMES. No bang, you mean.

DRAKE. Well yes.

JAMES. *Every* time? What about college? I thought everyone was at it there.

DRAKE. Everyone except me. I was too nervous. While I was doing theoretical physics they were all doing practical biology. Then I came to London and I thought things were looking up. The first real chance I had, it was the perfect set-up. The girl had her own flat.

JAMES. What went wrong?

DRAKE. I set it on fire. I was so impatient I grabbed her while the dinner was cooking. By the time we noticed what was happening, the Boeuf Bourgignon had turned to filet flambe.

JAMES. Have another drink. *(Pours.)* But there must have been others. I mean, what about all those birds at the studios? Presenters with hair down to their waist and dancers with legs up to their ...?

DRAKE. It makes no difference. I've tried the morning — the window cleaner arrives. The afternoon — Jehovah's Witnesses. Evening — burst pipe and the ceiling falls in. I've even come home and found some blighter in my ruddy bed.

JAMES. Oops — Cheers.

DRAKE. Three years you've been away, James, and you pick this one night to come back and pinch my most essential piece of furniture.

JAMES. I wish I was dead. It just seems so.... *Every* time?

DRAKE. Well, nearly every time. The few occasions nothing's happened, I'm so terrified something's going to happen, nothing happens!

JAMES. I think I follow that.

DRAKE. I tell you, Jim, by the time I get it, I'll be past it!

JAMES. I really am very sorry.

DRAKE. I'm unique. Everyone's at it except me.

JAMES. Mustn't upset yourself.

DRAKE. Even the school kids. They'll soon be taking it at GCSE!

JAMES. No, no....

DRAKE. I feel like a has-been who hasn't been where everyone else has been.

JAMES. I know what you need.

DRAKE. What's that?

JAMES. The oldest cure in the world.

DRAKE. Witch doctors?

JAMES. No.

DRAKE. Oh. *(Clicks.)* Ohhh!

JAMES. *(Nodding.)* I'll treat you for your birthday.

DRAKE. I've tried it.

JAMES. What happened?

DRAKE. She insisted on having the television on at the same time. Said it stopped her getting bored with her work.

JAMES. Did that matter?

DRAKE. I happened to be on screen at the time. Have you ever tried sex with yourself watching — it's very inhibiting.

JAMES. Do you mind if I give you a piece of brotherly advice, old man?

DRAKE. Please do.

JAMES. The harder you work at this sort of problem, the worse it becomes. I mean look at you tonight — exuding desperation at every pore. That scares the pants off any girl.

DRAKE. It hasn't yet.

JAMES. Well that's my point. Now let me tell you the secret of my success.

DRAKE. Are you successful?

JAMES. *(Filling the glasses.)* Well, let me put it this way. It's one reason I've come back. For a rest.

DRAKE. A rest?

JAMES. I'm exhausted.

DRAKE. Really? How do you do it?

JAMES. What I do is to make out I don't want it. So what happens?

DRAKE. You don't get it.

JAMES. No! That's the point. Women are perverse creatures. As soon as they sense you're not after them, *they* immediately come after *you. (MRS. FINNEY comes out behind them, and listens, unnoticed.)* So they take one look at me and they think they're safe. Dear, harmless old Jim Harris they cry — he hasn't got nasty lecherous intentions like other men. So they hurl themselves onto my lap, with their arms round my neck and their boobs heaving under my nose — and they ask me to *protect* them!

DRAKE. And do you?

JAMES. 'Course not! I try. Every time I say to myself — 'Right, Jim, this time you're going to be firm, be adamant.' But there she lies – all warm and shiny; you smell her perfume, and you look into those great innocent eyes, and you're lost. What can you do?

MRS. F. I'd suggest an operation.

JAMES. *(Looking at DRAKE's lips.)* That really is amazing the way you do that!

(DRAKE indicates MRS. FINNEY. JAMES looks round.)

MRS. F. *(To JAMES.)* Your ping pong table's made up.

JAMES. Thank you.

MRS. F. I'll see you in the morning. *(To DRAKE.)* I'll tell you something, Mr. Harris. Downstairs I've got five kids and a husband that hits the bottle, but they don't cause me half the worry you do. And now the mad monk has arrived, I can see the place is going to be turned into a stud-farm. *(She marches to the front door and turns.)* All I can say is the sooner you two hit the change of life the better.

(She exits.)

JAMES. You ought to have her put down, you know.

DRAKE. She's a warm and caring person underneath.

JAMES. How far do you have to dig?

DRAKE. Got a dreadful husband. I think she comes up here just to get away from him.

JAMES. Well, there you are. We've all got problems.

DRAKE. What am I going to do, Jim?

JAMES. Go to bed. *(They get up, and stand swaying for a moment.)* Do you get the impression we're the only static things in this room?

DRAKE. *(Looking at empty bottle.)* What's that stuff made from?

JAMES. Vintage sheep-dip. *(He clasps DRAKE to him.)* My little brother. My poor little virgin brother.

DRAKE. Hey, have you got a job?

JAMES. Nope.

DRAKE. How about being my manager.

JAMES. Manager?

DRAKE. S'bout all I haven't got.

JAMES. What do I manage?

DRAKE. Me.

JAMES. I hope the pay's good.

DRAKE. Ten per cent of what I earn.

JAMES. *(Grandly.)* Oh, I'll let you keep more than that.

DRAKE. See Julia in the morning. Tell her you're my manager.

JAMES. Julia?

DRAKE. Secretary.

JAMES. Ah yes, the one who doesn't.

DRAKE. That's the one. I got to go to bed now. Up early for rehearsal. G'night.

JAMES. God bless.

DRAKE. Good to see you again, Jim. Good ol' Jim.

(He clasps JAMES drunkenly to him)

JAMES. Yeah, yeah. *(Struggles free.)* Don't get carried away, in case fate doesn't interrupt us. I'll get my clothes. *(During the ensuing dialogue he attempts to collect his shoes, socks, trousers, shirt and jacket from the armchair while still keeping the bedcover wrapped round himself. He drops as many things as he picks up.)* It's lovely to be back home again. Is it true what they say now about England?

DRAKE. Wassat?

JAMES. It's full of strikers and idle layabouts.

DRAKE. Just about.

JAMES. Good. Sounds just the place for me. And don't you worry about your little problem.

DRAKE. Problem?

JAMES. The one I mustn't laugh at. We'll sort that out in no time. My little brother shall seever the sacrets of six ... sivver the seckr ... savor the secrets of sex!

DRAKE. Terrific. We'll take London apart, Jim. You and me.

JAMES. Ah no. Not me, old son. I'm recuperating. I'm going to find a nice quiet little girl who'll keep me warm and feed me till I'm fat as an elephant. *(By this time JAMES is in such confusion with his clothes that he gives up and dumps the lot. He staggers towards the spare room door holding a single sock. Stops and turns.)* Psst! Psst!

DRAKE. Not as much as you are.

JAMES. Have you told anyone?

DRAKE. What?

JAMES. That you're a virgin?

DRAKE. 'Course not.

JAMES. Why not?

DRAKE. I'm supposed to be one of London's most with-it bachelors. If everyone knew I was without it I'd be a laughing stock.

JAMES. Yes. *(Sniggers.)*

DRAKE. But it's not funny, Jim.

JAMES. No, no. It's not funny. It's definitely not funny. It's very, very unfunny....

(JAMES staggers into the spare room trying to stifle his laughter. The front door opens and MRS. FINNEY enters, followed by HONEY.)

MRS. F. Mr. Harris, you've got a visitor.

DRAKE. Honey!

MRS. F. Seems it isn't her day with machinery. I found her stuck in the lift this time. She's obviously not destined to get out of here tonight, so I've brought her back. Put her out with the rubbish in the morning.

(She exits.)

HONEY. Has your brother got to bed yet? *(He nods and indicates the spare room.)* Then let's make sure he stays in it. *(Goes to spare room door, locks it, and returns.)* Well, lover boy, ready for me then? *(He nods eagerly. She holds out her arms.)* Well here I am!

(He tries to go towards her, but his feet are frozen.)

DRAKE. *(Hopelessly.)* Not again fate!

(He passes out falling flat on his face.)

CURTAIN

Scene 2

(The same. The following morning. The telephone is ringing. James's clothes still lie on the floor and the bed is well rumpled. The curtains are open and bright sunlight streams in. The flat door opens and MRS. FINNEY enters with a vacuum cleaner. She is also carrying a large bundle of mail. She presses a button and revolves the desk in.)

MRS. F. Telephones! How I hate telephones! *(To the phone.)* Belt up! *(She picks up the receiver, and answers in a smart telephone voice.)* Good morning! The Draycott Harris residence. No, I'm afraid Mr. Harris is at the television studios. *(Looks at watch.)* His secretary isn't here yet. Well I'm afraid he's booked up months ahead with all sorts of charities and good works. And then with the show and everything it's only Sundays he has free, and by the time he's attended Matins, Evensong and Confession he hasn't much time left.

(JULIA enters through the flat door. She is in her early twenties and very efficient. Her prettiness is somewhat disguised by her rather austere dress and hair style. She wears glasses.)

JULIA. *(Brightly business-like.)* Good morning, Mrs. Finney.
MRS. F. *(On phone.)* 'Ang on, his secretary's 'ere. *(Corrects herself.)* I mean Miss Carrington has just arrived. *(To JULIA.)* It's the Wargrave Women's Institute or something.

(JULIA takes the phone.)

JULIA. *(To MRS. FINNEY.)* Did Draycott leave for the studios on time?
MRS. F. Dunno. I've only just arrived.

(She gets on with making the bed.)

JULIA. *(On phone.)* Good morning, Julia Carrington speaking....

Attend your Christmas Fete!... Ah, no. *(Refers to diary.)* He hasn't really a spare moment until August next year — you couldn't hold it then, could you? No. I'm afraid I can't suggest anybody else who might be free.

MRS. F. Try Bill Clinton.

JULIA. *(On phone.)* A pleasure. Good-bye. *(She replaces receiver.)* A lot of mail this morning, Mrs. Finney.

MRS. F. The usual number of marriage proposals no doubt.

JULIA. Pathetic women!

(She sits at desk and goes through the mail.)

MRS. F. Well, if he carries on the rate he's going there won't be much of him left to marry. You should have seen what was going on here last ....

JULIA. *(Interrupting.)* I don't want to listen to any of your gossip, thank you, Mrs. Finney.

MRS. F. Me. Gossip? I know you wouldn't hear a thing against him.

JULIA. I'm perfectly well aware of Draycott's shortcomings. However, what he does in his private life is no concern of ours.

MRS. F. All right, all right. Then I won't tell you about the girl he had here last night. *(Demonstrates.)* She had the sexiest ....

JULIA. Mrs. Finney!

MRS. F. No, she didn't.

(The telephone rings and JULIA answers it.)

JULIA. Harris Enterprises. Ah, good morning. Isn't he? *(To MRS. FINNEY.)* It's the studio. He hasn't arrived yet.

MRS. F. *(Looking at her watch.)* Hasn't he?

JULIA. *(On phone.)* Well, I'm sure he's on his way.

MRS. F. Via Buenos Aires probably.

JULIA. *(Ignoring this.)* I'll see what I can find out. I expect he'll be with you any moment, fresh as a daisy. *(At that moment the bathroom door opens and DRAYCOTT comes out looking like a zombie. He stands swaying, half-conscious. He wears the same clothes that he had on the night before, now decidedly crumpled and minus his shoes. His hair is a mess.)* Fine. Let me know if he arrives. Good morning. *(Sees DRAKE.)* Good God! *(To phone.)* Goodbye. *(She replaces receiver and goes to DRAKE followed by MRS. FINNEY. They support him on either side.)* Are you all right, Draycott?

DRAKE. Mmm?

JULIA. Are you feeling all right?

MRS. F. That's a bloody silly question.

JULIA. Draycott, are you ill?

MRS. F. 'Course he's not ill. He's still half pissed. My old man looks like that every morning.

JULIA. Oh, for heavens sake!

MRS. F. I told you he was busy last night. He'll look pretty on the box tonight, won't he?

JULIA. Draycott, it's ten o'clock.

DRAKE. *(Heading for the bed.)* Good, I'll get an early night.

(He crawls onto the bed. JULIA follows.)

JULIA. Why aren't you at the studios?

DRAKE. Just wanna sleep.

JULIA. They've phoned to find out where you are.

DRAKE. Where who is?

JULIA. *(Exasperated.)* Oh, pull yourself together!

(She pulls him up into a sitting position.)

MRS. F. Come on, walk him up and down like they do in the films.

(They haul him off the bed, each put one of his arms round their shoulders and march him smartly up and down.)

JULIA. Do you think we should get a doctor?

MRS. F. It's not a doctor he needs, it's a vet. Come on — left, right, left, right, left right....

(They go at almost a run backwards and forwards across the room,

and eventually come to a breathless stop.)

DRAKE. *(Panting.)* Have we got there?
JULIA. We'll stick his head under the cold tap. Bring him through.

(She abandons MRS. FINNEY and goes into the bathroom.)

MRS. F. Hey, hold on.... *(DRAKE swings round to hang round her neck.)* Now come on, Mr. Harris. *(With difficulty she struggles with his inert body, then lifts his legs so that he is standing on her own feet.)* Right, that's it. Here we go. Slow, slow, quick, quick slow.

(She waltzes off with him into the bathroom. The phone rings. JULIA re-enters.)

JULIA. *(Over her shoulder.)* Keep his head under water until he wakes up or drowns. *(To phone.)* Harris Enterprises? Cooks? Oh, Tooks. Good morning, Miss Tooks, how do you do. I'm Mr. Harris's secretary, Julia Carrington.... Yes I'm looking forward to meeting you too. I'm afraid your first day on the team hasn't got off to a good start.... I know he's not at the studio. He's here — that's the problem.... I think the best thing is for you to get over here right away and then take him back with you. He, er ... he's got a slight headache. I expect he was working late last night and overdid it. Pardon? I thought you said something.... Well would you tell the producer he's fine and will be there as soon as possible? Thank you. We'll have him all ready when you arrive. 'Bye.

(She replaces the receiver and starts to move towards the bathroom. The spare room door handle rattles. She stops and stares. There are loud thumps on the door. She unlocks it and a disheveled JAMES rushes out still wrapped in the bedcover.)

JAMES. Thanks, old man, I'm bursting for a .... *(Stops on seeing JULIA.)* Good Lord, another one!
JULIA. What?

JAMES. Which bit of the furniture did you crawl out of?

JULIA. *(Indignant.)* Are you a friend of Mr. Harris's?

JAMES. No — er — yes, I am. I'm also his brother. *(Indicates bathroom.)* Do you think I could....

JULIA. I thought you were abroad.

JAMES. No, I'm a feller. Oh, I see. Yes, I am.... I was. I'm back. *(Shakes hands.)* James Harris. How do you do? Do you think I could....

JULIA. Are you the reason for his condition this morning?

JAMES. Well, I, er ... I .... D'you you think I could go to the bathroom first?

(He hurries to the bathroom just as MRS. FINNEY comes out.)

MRS. F. *(Into his face.)* Oh, you!

JAMES. *(Holding his head.)* Oh God!

MRS. F. You're the reason for the state of him!

JAMES. If you'll excuse me, I'm just, er .... *(Indicating JULIA.)* Who is that?

MRS. F. Mr. Harris's secretary.

JAMES. Oh, the one who doesn't.

JULIA. Pardon?

JAMES. *(Hurriedly.)* Excuse me.

(JAMES exits into bathroom.)

JULIA. Just what was going on in here last night?

MRS. F. Everything but full frontal lap dancing.

JULIA. And *you* were here?

MRS. F. Only directing the traffic.

JULIA. I suppose the traffic included girls?

MRS. F. I thought you weren't interested?·

JULIA. I'm not.

MRS. F. Well, it was one girl actually. She was ... and she was ....

(MRS. F. attempts to demonstrate Honey's shape with gestures).

JULIA. Oh, he's such a fool!

(JAMES re-enters from tile bathroom.)

JAMES. I'm a bit worried about Draycott. He's fast asleep with his head in the basin of water.
MRS. F. Oh, lawd!

(MRS. FINNEY exits to the bathroom.)

JAMES. He looks as bad as I feel.
JULIA. He deserves to. He has no right to behave like that with a show to get on.
JAMES. We only had one small bottle between us.
JULIA. What was in it, rat poison?
JAMES. Australian schnapps.
JULIA. What?
JAMES. One sip and you're down-under.

(MRS. FINNEY re-enters.)

MRS. F. I've pulled him out. And I've left him with six Alka Selzas and a glass of Andrews.
JAMES. Well at least we'll know where to find him.
MRS. F. I'll get some coffee on.
JAMES. Just what I need.
MRS. F. For him!
JAMES. Pardon me for living.
MRS. F. I'll have to consider that.
JAMES. Look, you may as well get used to having me here. I'm his new manager.
JULIA. Manager?
JAMES. That's right.
MRS. F. Julia's his manager.
JAMES. Julia's his *secretary*.
JULIA. I see.
JAMES. Don't worry, there aren't going to be any immediate re-

dundancies.

MRS. F. Uh!

JAMES. *(Glaring at her.)* On second thought ....

MRS. F. Look, you may be his manager but you can't go around in his soft furnishings all day. Come on, give me back that bedcover.

(She grabs at it.)

JAMES. Gerroff!

MRS. F. Let's have it.

(MRS. FINNEY tries to pull it off.)

JAMES. Get off me, you sex maniac!

MRS. F. *(Letting go, outraged.)* Oo! Ooo!

JAMES. Get in there and make the coffee.

MRS. F. I'll give you sex!

JAMES. Wait 'till you're asked. *(MRS. FINNEY exits into the kitchen, furious.)* They should make a film about her — 'Alien Five'!

JULIA. Will you excuse the secretary if she gets on with her work? Perhaps the manager can get Draycott dressed.

(JULIA sits at desk.)

JAMES. I must say he looks in a bad way.

JULIA. We'll all be in a bad way if he loses his job. *(She furiously starts to type.)* It's all so pathetic! You'd never think so, but he really has talent! Some of his interviews are terrific. You realize the program's always in the Top Ten. He's had everyone on it, from the Prime Minister to Miss World.

JAMES. Naturally.

JULIA. *(Holding out a sheet.)* File that under Income Tax Returns.

JAMES. Hold on — I'm not going to ....

JULIA. You work here don't you?

JAMES. Well, yes but ....

JULIA. Then make yourself useful!

JAMES. Right.

(He takes the sheet and looks around for the filing cabinet as she carries on typing.)

JULIA. Now's the time he should be developing his talent. He should be working himself to the bone. He should be putting all he's got into widening his scope, expanding his career. *(Holds out a letter.)* And file this under Fan Mail. Here! *(JAMES takes it and searches desperately for the filing cabinet. During this next speech JULIA goes on furiously talking and typing while he tries to ask her where to file the items, but he can't get a word in. In despair he presses one of the buttons on the control button. He sends JULIA revolving round still typing and talking. He frantically jumps on the revolve as she goes round, revolves once himself, jumps off again, presses a button and finally stops it on her second time around. She hands him the copy of the letter and starts to type a third letter. JAMES is still trying to spot where the filing cabinet is. Finally he finds the correct button, and the filing cabinet appears from the other wall.)* Whew!

JULIA. And he writes too. Have you read his articles?

JAMES. No, er ....

JULIA. He's had stuff printed in *The Spectator, Newsweek, Time Magazine*.... But why stop there? Oh damn! *(She has made a mistake in her typing so whips the paper out.)* Wastepaper basket! *(JAMES dashes for the basket and returns just in time to field the screwed up letter she hurls towards him. He then throws the other letters in the basket while she goes on talking and re-typing the third letter.)* Life is just a game for him. One long round of late nights and girls, girls, girls, girls, girls.

JAMES. Girls?

JULIA. Blonde ones, brown ones, long ones, short ones, he doesn't mind. What's the address of the Variety Club?

JAMES. I don't know.

JULIA. S to Z telephone directory.

JAMES. Er, yes, I'll ....

(The telephone rings.)

JULIA. Answer it.

JAMES Er, what about the ....

JULIA. *(Pressing on still.)* I don't know how I've stood it all this time....

JAMES. Shall I answer the, er — or get the, er .... I'll get the, er....

(He goes and gets the telephone directory.)

JULIA. I can't imagine anybody else putting up with it. A girl has only got to stick her chest in front of him and he's a goner. Answer the phone, will you?

JAMES. I was getting the, er .... *(Lifts the receiver.)* The Draycott Harris madhouse....Yes, she is. Who is it, please?

JULIA. File that under 'Contracts.'

(She thrusts a letter at JAMES.)

JAMES. Er, yes.... *(To phone.)* One moment. *(To JULIA.)* It's the *TV Times*.

(He's still got the directory and the waste basket, so he puts the telephone between his legs to take the letter and hands the receiver to JULIA.)

JULIA. *(To phone.)* 'Morning. . . Fine, would you read it to me, please? *(She walks round the room listening on the receiver, with JAMES following her round with the phone between his legs, clutching everything else.)* Yes.... Good.... Yes.... Fine.... Very good.... Yes, you can print that.

(She yanks the phone from between JAMES's legs, replaces the receiver and puts phone on desk. JAMES doubles up with pain.)

JAMES. *(Finally.)* I think I've been disconnected!

(She has taken no notice and has returned to her angry typing, muttering to herself.)

JULIA. Have you got that address yet?
JAMES. I was just ....
JULIA. And I want some envelopes, please. Large ones.
JAMES. Yes, I'll just find the, er ....

(He carries on searching in the directory.)

JULIA. Instead of working he lets himself be diverted by every dolly bird who appears. Where's that address??

(JAMES in despair rips the page from the directory and slaps it on the desk.)

JAMES. It's on that page somewhere!

(With JULIA still talking he throws the letter he is holding into the basket and crosses to find envelopes.)

JULIA. I try, I really do. *(Indicates desk drawer.)* Envelopes are here! *(He does a 'U' turn.)* I do my best to keep him focussed. Make him concentrate on the things that matter, but I can't keep up. File that under 'Charities'. I just can't keep up.
JAMES. *(Obeying)* I know how you feel.
JULIA. Put one of his photos in each of the envelopes.
JAMES. One of his photos ....
JULIA. In each of the envelopes. It's fan mail.
JAMES. Where will I find his photos?
JULIA. Filing cabinet.
JAMES. Under ...?
JULIA. Photos!
JAMES. Ask a silly question ....

(He dashes to the files, finds the photos and, machine-like, sticks them in the envelopes.)

JULIA. *(Pressing on.)* Just when I think I'm winning, in will float some tight bottomed, loose topped female, and he's gone catatonic again! It's not fair. It really isn't. *(She is nearly in tears.)* But I refuse to let it upset me anymore. I refuse! Tissues, please!

JAMES. Don't tell me — filed under Tissues.

(JAMES gets the tissues from the filing cabinet, hands her one, and during the next speech stands beside her listening and inadvertently putting the tissues in the envelopes instead of the photos.)

JULIA. And not content with his daytime activities, he has to go on the rampage all night as well. And then he's no use to anyone. Least of all himself. *(JAMES hands her a tissue, she blows her nose on it, hands it back and he puts it in an envelope.)* Look at the state he's in this morning! Hopeless! Stick the stamps on. *(She hands a page of stamps to him. JAMES starts to stick the stamps on the envelope.)* He's obviously been at it all night long. With some big-busted, bird-brained .... *(Turns to JAMES.)* Who brought her here — YOU?! *(JAMES is so surprised by this attack that he half swallows the stamp he's licking. While she continues talking and typing he fishes in his mouth and eventually manages to cough it up and retrieve it.)* Not that it would matter to him where she came from. Why does he do it? I don't understand him. I've tried to understand him. I *want* to understand him. What's the *matter* with him?

(She bursts into floods of tears. JAMES sticks the stamp on the tissue box, puts it in the in-tray and throws the photos in the waste basket. He puts a consoling arm around JULIA who clutches him and buries her head in his stomach.)

JAMES. *(Embarrassed.)* Now, look here, you mustn't ....

(DRAKE staggers out of the bathroom looking a little better.)

DRAKE. Good morning.
JAMES. You bastard!
DRAKE. Good-bye.

(He revolves in one movement and goes back into bathroom.)

JULIA. *(Recovering.)* I'm sorry.
JAMES. That's all right.

(She mops his front with a tissue. The entry phone buzzer goes.)

JULIA. Pull him out of the bathroom and get him into some proper clothes, will you?

(JAMES heads for the bathroom as MRS. FINNEY comes out of the kitchen with a tray of coffee mugs.)

JAMES. *(To her.)* Does every morning here start off like this?
MRS. F. Sundays are worse.
JULIA. *(To entry phone.)* Hullo.
HONEY. *(Over speaker.)* It's me. Honey Tooks.
JULIA. Push the door Miss Tooks.
MRS. F. Coffee up.
JULIA. *(To entry phone.)* The lift's facing you. Penthouse flat, top floor.
HONEY. Thank you.

(JAMES enters from the bathroom supporting DRAKE.)

MRS. F. Batman and Robin.
DRAKE. My head feels dreadful.
JAMES. It looks worse.
MRS. F. Here you are — a cup of coffee.
JAMES. Oh, thanks.
MRS. F. Who mentioned you?

(MRS. FINNEY gives the mug to DRAKE.)

MRS. F. Julia?
JULIA. No thanks. Now listen, Draycott — Honey Tooks is on her way up ....
JAMES. Is it bed-time, already?
JULIA. She's his new PR girl.

JAMES. Ah — yes, of course.

MRS. F. *(To JAMES.)* I suppose you want some?

JAMES. Yes please. *(She grudgingly gives him a mug of coffee.)* Thanks. Oh, it's black! *(MRS. FINNEY glares ferociously.)* I like it black.

(MRS. FINNEY exits to the spare room.)

JULIA. Come on, now Drake. *(Hands him a file.)* Here's the script for tonight's show. Get into some decent clothes and go to the studios with Honey Tooks. And please keep your hands off her.

DRAKE. What's that supposed to mean?

JULIA. *(To JAMES.)* I'll hold you responsible.

JAMES. *(Loftily.)* My client will keep his private life and his Public Relations quite separate.

JULIA. Your client would happily take his private life into Trafalgar Square and have public relations amongst the pigeons!

(She exits kitchen.)

JAMES. I must say for a virgin you've got a hell of a reputation!

DRAKE. And for someone who's trying to give it up you've got a hell of a nerve. Didn't take you long to wrap yourself round my secretary.

JAMES. I was giving her a helping hand.

DRAKE. Looked more like a helping bellyful to me.

JAMES. *(Furious.)* She needed a shoulder to cry on!

DRAKE. *(Ditto.)* You keep your shoulder in a very funny place!

JAMES. *(Deflating.)* They're hard to find — I can't help my shape. I'll get your clothes. *(JAMES has a guess at another button, and out swings the wardrobe.)* Bingo!

(He selects a jacket and pair of trousers.)

DRAKE. What was she crying about anyway?

JAMES. You.

DRAKE. Me?

JAMES. Yes, you.

DRAKE. *(Puzzled.)* That can't be it.

JAMES. How d'you know? I got most of it.

DRAKE. Ah! I know what's bothering her.

JAMES. So do I, chum. What bothers most girls at her age. And most men all their lives.

DRAKE. Julia's not interested in sex.

JAMES. *(Derisively.)* Oh, blimey!

DRAKE. All she cares about is her job. The Draycott Harris Show. That's what she was upset about.

JAMES. The girl's in love with you.

DRAKE. In love with me! She spends her entire life nagging at me.

JAMES. That's what I said. She loves you.

DRAKE. *(Shaking his head.)* I don't get it.

JAMES. Well you haven't had it.

DRAKE. Anyway for God's sake don't let her know my new P.R. girl was up here last night or my life won't be worth living. *(The flat front door bell rings.)* That's Honey now! *(Struggles with the zip of his trousers.)* Quick - help me get these things off.

JAMES. I should shake hands first. Oh, I see what you mean.

(JAMES takes the new trousers off the hanger, while DRAKE undoes the trousers he's wearing. JULIA comes out of kitchen and opens the front door. HONEY comes in. She looks startling even in her 'working' clothes, which are a trouser suit and a large hat.)

HONEY. Good morning. You must be Julia.

JULIA. *(Taken aback.)* Yes. Are you Honey Tooks?

HONEY. Yes. Lovely to meet ....

(She tails off as she sees DRAKE, who is standing there with his trousers half off.)

JULIA. You've met Draycott Harris, haven't you?

HONEY. *(Innocently.)* Briefly. *(Comes forward.)* Good morning Mr. Harris. *(Aside.)* Not now darling!

(She places her hat strategically in front of him.)

DRAKE. *(Zipping up his trousers.)* Good morning.
JULIA. Have you met his brother, James?
HONEY. Yes.
DRAKE. *(Quickly.)* No!
HONEY. No?
JAMES. No.
HONEY. No. How do you do?
JAMES. How do you do.
DRAKE. James is my new manager.
HONEY. That's convenient.
JULIA. We haven't got much time. *(Gets folder from desk.)* If you could take him through the show, I'll get some breakfast together.
JAMES. Oh good, I'm starving ....
JULIA. Not for you, for him.
JAMES. Naturally.

(JULIA thrusts the folder into DRAKE's hand and exits into kitchen.)

HONEY. Well, well, well. We are in a state, aren't we? *(To DRAKE.)* What happened? I left you for dead last night.
JAMES. Last night? You went home.
HONEY. I came back.
JAMES. You don't give up, do you?
HONEY. No but he does. He took one look at me and passed out.
JAMES. Well, he hasn't come to yet. *(Dumps the new clothes in her arms.)* There's his clothes. Get him ready.
HONEY. I thought you were the manager.
JAMES. That's right. I'm going to see if I can manage to get myself dressed. *(The telephone rings. JAMES answers.)* The Draycott Harris Menagerie. His manager speaking. *(To DRAKE.)* It's the editor of *Women's Own*.
DRAKE. *Women's Own*?
JAMES. She wants to know if you'll write a celebrity article on your attitude towards sex. *(To phone.)* Which issue is it for? Next week's? He might have something to say by the week after.

(He puts the phone down and goes into bathroom.)

HONEY. Come on, get your trousers off.

(She tries to pull his trousers off while he's still concentrating on his script. JAMES returns toweling his face. He watches for a brief second.)

JAMES. Is this a game for two, or can anyone join in?
HONEY. Don't just stand there — help!
JAMES. All right.

(He throws his towel down and goes to help.)

HONEY. Trousers first.
JAMES. Whatever you say.

(He unzips her trousers.)

HONEY. His!
JAMES. *(To DRAKE as he rips off his trousers.)* I warn you, I shall want more pay for this. I didn't expect managing you meant being doctor, valet, and nappy-changer as well. *(To HONEY.)* You can do the rest. I'm going to get dressed myself.

(He heads for the spare room.)

HONEY. You can't leave me to manage him on my own.
JAMES. *(Indicating DRAKE, standing there in his under shorts.)* Don't complain. You've got a lot farther than you did last time. *(Opens the spare room door.)* Oh. Mrs. Finney, can I have this room please. I want to get dressed.
MRS. F. *(Appearing.)* Why can't you get dressed in...? *(Sees DRAKE with HONEY kneeling at his feet and his trousers round his ankles.)* Bloody hell!
JAMES. We're all trying to get dressed. *(To MRS. FINNEY.)* Please knock if you want to come in.

MRS. F. I've seen it all before, you know.
JAMES. What a good memory you have.

(JAMES goes out. MRS. FINNEY comes down to HONEY as JULIA comes out of the kitchen with a breakfast tray.)

MRS. F. What's going on here? *(Peers at HONEY.)* Oh it's you.
JULIA. *(Surprised.)* Have you met Honey Tooks?
MRS. F. Yes.
HONEY. No!
MRS. F. No?
DRAKE. No.
MRS. F. No.
DRAKE. *(Pointedly.)* Mrs. Finney, Honey is here on *business.*

(MRS. FINNEY roars with laughter.)

MRS. F. *(Stopping.)* I beg your pardon.

(She goes into the kitchen while DRAKE gets dressed.)

JULIA. *(Putting tray on coffee table.)* Here you are. Some boiled eggs and toast. You need something proper to eat. Right, Honey, if you'll shove some of that breakfast down him, I'll go and get a taxi for you. *(To DRAKE angrily.)* And for heaven's sake try and grow up! There are other things in life besides birds and booze! And I know it's not my place to tell you but someone's got to! And don't think I'm upset because I'm not!

(She bursts into tears, and exits by the front door.)

HONEY. I think she rather fancies you herself.
DRAKE. Not you too. Why is everyone trying to get me off with my secretary.
HONEY. Well, you get off with everyone else.
DRAKE. *(Scratching his head.)* It's amazing how that rumor's

got around.

(He returns to his script as JAMES comes out of the spare room, fully dressed.)

HONEY. Ah, that's better.
JAMES. What is?
HONEY. You look quite attractive with your clothes on.
JAMES. Thank you. You're quite a transformation yourself.
HONEY. It's my professional front. It's supposed to intimidate people.
JAMES. It scares the hell out of me. *(Looking hopefully at the tray.)* Do I see breakfast?
HONEY. It's for Draycott.
JAMES. Oh. *(Wistful.)* Looks nice.
DRAKE. Help yourself. I'm not hungry.
JAMES. Thank you.

(Picks up the tray and heads for the bathroom.)

HONEY. Where are you taking it?
JAMES. The bathroom. Seems to be the only place left.
HONEY. *(Catching his trouser waist.)* Don't be silly. Stay and have it here.
JAMES. I'd rather not. I've caused enough trouble between you two.
HONEY. But there isn't anywhere to sit in there.
JAMES. Yes there is and it's very comfortable.
HONEY. *(Hauling him by the waist.)* I insist. You sit there. Move up, Draycott. *(She puts JAMES onto the settee next to DRAKE and then sits on the arm next to JAMES.)* There we are. Shall I be mum. Coffee, Draycott. James. *(She leans forward, her cleavage right in front of JAMES.)* Sugar?
JAMES. *(Trying not to look.)* Two lumps.
HONEY. *(Putting sugar in with sugar tongs.)* One. Two.
JAMES. Perfect.
HONEY. Milk?

JAMES. *(Hastily.)* No, thanks!

(She gives him his coffee and, much to his relief, leans back. JAMES moves away, crowding DRAKE who is sipping his coffee.)

DRAKE. *(Irritably.)* I'm finding this a bit overcrowded.

JAMES. Sorry, old man. I'll just have a quick bite ... *(He turns away to come face to face with HONEY'S cleavage again.)* ... and then I'll be gone.

HONEY. Don't spoil your digestion.

JAMES. It's not my digestion I'm worried about. *(He picks up a thin slice of toast)* Ah, soldiers!

HONEY. You know, you're actually rather sweet, James.

JAMES. Thank you.

HONEY. Don't you think so, Draycott?

DRAKE. Adorable. Just let him get on with his breakfast. *(To JAMES.)* And you — get on with it!

(He nudges JAMES's elbow which results in his teaspoon going down HONEY's cleavage. JAMES is at a loss to know what to do. HONEY stares at him blankly. He tries to pluck up courage to take it out with his fingers, but finally uses the sugar tongs. The spoon comes out bent double [alternative spoon]. He stares at it, eyes wide.)

HONEY. Definitely adorable.

JAMES. Look, leave me alone, will you?

HONEY. *(Sighing.)* All right. What are you doing after the show tonight, Drake?

DRAKE. Tonight? I think I ought to get to bed early.

HONEY. Fine. Come and do it at my place. *(JAMES chokes on his egg.)* Did you say something?

JAMES. No. As his manager I'm all for it. I won't even ask for my ten percent.

HONEY. *(To DRAKE.)* That's settled then. You come straight back to my place after the show and I'll have something tasty for you. *(JAMES chokes again.)* Will you be able to entertain yourself for the evening, James?

JAMES. I'll manage.

HONEY. Then perhaps I can entertain you some other time.

DRAKE. Look, do you mind keeping your sights on one target at a time?

HONEY. *(Beaming.)* All right. Let's have a quick volley now then.

(She kisses him heartily just as JULIA walks in. She stops dead.)

JULIA. Oh!

JAMES. Cease fire!

(Takes his tray smartly to the desk. They break hastily apart.)

JULIA. *(Furiously)* Oh ... oh ...!

HONEY. Please don't be angry, Julia. It was just ....

JULIA. Oh!

HONEY. I promise, it wasn't ....

JULIA. I'm so sorry, Honey!

HONEY. Eh?

JULIA. *(Furious, to DRAKE.)* Even when he's half dead on his feet, he's still capable of assault.

DRAKE. *(Stunned.)* Me?

JULIA. You're unbelievable! *Anyone's* fair game to you. Even your own PR girl when she's on the job!

HONEY. Well, I wasn't quite.

JULIA. Well that's the final straw! I'm giving in a fortnight's notice. And you owe me two weeks holiday, so that means I'm leaving tonight with a month's salary!

DRAKE. Julia, you don't understand.

JULIA. Oh yes I do! *(To JAMES.)* And what are you doing here?

JAMES. *(Innocently.)* Would you believe me if I said I was just having my breakfast?

JULIA. No.

JAMES. There's not much point in saying anything then, is there?

JULIA. *(To DRAKE.)* Well now that you've obviously revived, I'm sure you'll be able to get downstairs to the taxi. If you have any trouble from him in the lift, Honey, press the alarm bell and hit him with the fire extinguisher.

(MRS. FINNEY comes out of the kitchen with a vacuum cleaner.)

MRS. F. Are they still here?

JULIA. They're just leaving.

MRS. F. Good. It's like trying to mow the pitch while the game's on, this place. *(To HONEY.)* And will you be coming back late again tonight?

HONEY. *(Casting a look at JULIA.)* Er ....

MRS. F. Because if so, I'd better show you how to work the lift.

DRAKE. *(Urgent.)* Mrs. Finney ....

JULIA. *(Frowning.)* Work the lift?

MRS. F. Yes, she jammed up the whole works last night. Or rather this morning. It was practically dawn by the time .... *(She realizes the situation.)* Well, it gets light very early now doesn't it.... I'll just go and rinse this under the tap.

(She indicates vacuum cleaner and exits to the kitchen. Everyone waits for JULIA's stunned reaction.)

JULIA. *(To HONEY.)* What were you doing here last night?

HONEY. Er ....

JULIA. *(To DRAKE.)* What was she doing here last night?

DRAKE. Er ....

JULIA. *(To JAMES.)* What was she doing here last night?

JAMES. Spot of overtime?

JULIA. *(Turning to DRAKE.)* Tell me, Draycott — what was she doing here last night?

DRAKE. *(To JAMES, whispering.)* James, do something.

JAMES. Eh?

DRAKE. Do something!

JAMES. *(Stepping forward.)* There was a young man from Madras ....

DRAKE. Oh shut up! Julia, nothing happened between us.

JULIA. *(Aloof.)* You don't have to explain to me.

DRAKE. No, you're right. I don't! What business is it of yours anyway? You don't even work for me anymore.

JULIA. Yes, I do. Until five o'clock.

DRAKE. No you don't. I'm firing you as from now.

JULIA. You can't do that.

DRAKE. Oh yes I can!

JULIA. No you can't

JAMES. *(Stepping forward.)* As his manager ....

JULIA. Shut up!

JAMES. *(Stepping back.)* Right.

HONEY. *(Dragging DRAKE off.)* Come along, Draycott — rehearsals. We'll see you later Julia.

JULIA. No you won't. At five o'clock I'm finished for good.

DRAKE. I want you in at ten a.m. sharp tomorrow morning, Julia.

JULIA. Why? You won't even be dressed and sober at that time.

JAMES. Speaking as his manager ....

HONEY. Shut up!

JAMES. Right.

(Everyone starts talking at once.)

HONEY. I think you're being a bit naive you know Julia. After all he is an adult and ... *(etc)*.

DRAKE. Will you please all stop shouting. I've got a splitting headache, I feel sick and I've a lot to do ... *(etc)*.

JULIA. Honey, will you please keep out of this. It has absolutely nothing to do with you. I have been working for Draycott Harris for two years and ....

JAMES. *(Stepping forward.)* I would just like to say ....

HONEY, DRAKE and JULIA. *(All together.)* SHUT UP!

JAMES. Right. *(DRAKE yanks HONEY out of the front door after him and slams the door. Pause.)* Phew! Just a normal day at the office.

JULIA. *(Turning on JAMES.)* This is all your fault, isn't it?

JAMES. Oh, do me a favor!

JULIA. You were here last night. You knew she was the one. I bet you encouraged it.

JAMES. I was just an innocent bystander. That sort of woman scares me to death. She's a man-eater.

JULIA. Well she was certainly making a good breakfast out of you two!

JAMES. Now look ....

JULIA. Which meal is she planning next, I wonder.

JAMES. Dinner actually.

JULIA. What?

JAMES. Oh dear. I don't think I should have said that.

JULIA. Dinner?

JAMES. Well, yes.

JULIA. Tonight?

JAMES. Well, yes.

JULIA. Where?

JAMES. Well I don't think I should ....

JULIA. Where?

JAMES. I'm not telling!

JULIA. *(Fiercely, raising a paper knife.)* Where?

JAMES. *(Quickly.)* Her place.

JULIA. I certainly *am* naive. Your brother's just taking advantage of me.

JAMES. *(Muttering.)* Well if he isn't, it's high time he did.

JULIA. *(Almost in tears.)* Oh, how I despise that man! Do you hear James? I despise him! *(Goes to the kitchen door.)* Mrs. Finney, I despise ...! *(As she opens the door, MRS. FINNEY falls in on her knees with a clatter of dustpan and brush, having been listening at door. She pretends to brush the carpet.)* I despise Draycott Harris!

MRS. F. *(Getting to her feet, deadpan.)* Yes, dear.

JULIA. I absolutely and utterly despise him!

JAMES. Isn't it time you stopped saying that?

JULIA. What?

JAMES. Nobody believes it. Except perhaps Drake. You certainly don't believe it.

JULIA. I certainly do.

JAMES. Well, *we* don't believe it, do we Mrs. Finney?

MRS. F. No.

JULIA. *(To MRS. FINNEY.)* Don't you?

MRS. F. Lord, no.

JULIA. How *do* I feel about him then?

MRS. F. I don't know, dear, but you get so worked up about how he spends his nights, there's only one way to find out.

JULIA. What's that?

MRS. F. Spend one with him, and see if it's worth the worry.

(JULIA is stunned.)

JULIA. *(Finally to JAMES.)* Did you hear that?

JAMES. Yes. I think we talk the same language after all.

JULIA. *(To MRS. FINNEY.)* If you're suggesting I'm in love with Draycott ....

MRS. F. Ah, now I didn't say anything about love, dear. People spend half their time these days talking about love, when what they're really worried about is sex. Sex is like food. If you haven't had any for a long time, you can think of nothing else. If you have it regular, as is natural, you get it over, clear the table, and get on with more important things. As an expert, wouldn't you agree, Mr. Harris?

JAMES. Don't ask me — I'm on a diet.

MRS. F. Now your boss is quite a palatable dish. You fancy him, that's obvious, or you wouldn't be so worried about who else is having a nibble. But if I were you I should get a move on while there's still something left on the plate.

(She exits into kitchen.)

JAMES. *(Calling after her.)* Thank you, Delia Smith!

JULIA. *(Outraged.)* If you think I'd throw myself at.... If the idea is for me to actually try to.... How would I go about it?

JAMES. How does any girl go about it?

JULIA. But this is different. Bosses don't go to bed with their secretaries.

(JAMES looks up to heaven in disbelief.)

JAMES. Oh, save me!
JULIA. Well, anyway, there's another slight problem.
JAMES. What's that?
JULIA. I've never actually.... Well, gone the whole . I'm still, what you call it? — intacta.
JAMES. In where? *(Realizing.)* Oh! *(Sympathetically.)* Ahhh! *(Thinking of DRAKE.)* Ooo!

(He doubles up laughing.)

JULIA. It's nothing to laugh about.
JAMES. *(Roaring.)* So I'm told!
JULIA. And Drake is practically a professional at it. *(JAMES is hysterical.)* Anyway, he's going round to Honey's tonight so that's that.
JAMES. Well, if you really want him, find her someone else.
JULIA. Who?
JAMES. A substitute. Anyone in trousers will do her. Don't you know any fancy-free bachelors?
JULIA. *(Thoughtful.)* Yes....
JAMES. There you are then.
JULIA. What are you doing tonight?
JAMES. Nothing. All you've got to do is promise him a good time and send him round.... *(Realizing)* Oh, no! *(He backs away from her.)* Julia, I'm trying to give it up.
JULIA. Please, James.
JAMES. She's not my type. She terrifies me. I could never stand the pace. I'm a protected species!
JULIA. Please!

(She has backed him towards the kitchen door just as MRS. FINNEY comes out with a cup of tea.)

JAMES. Mrs. Finney, the girl's insane. She wants *me* to go round to Honey's instead of Drake. I mean, tell her.... I'm not up to it. I couldn't, could I — a man in my state? Have you seen my state? *(Despairing.)* Mrs. Finney, *say* something!

    MRS. F. *(Toasting him with tea-cup.)* Bottoms up!

(JAMES hurries out of the flat door pursued by JULIA.)

CURTAIN

ACT II

Scene 1

(That evening. The curtains are drawn, and the lights are pleasantly low. The furniture is arranged in its domestic positions, except for the bed, which is up. The coffee table is laid for dinner for two, with a small candelabra as a centerpiece.

As the CURTAIN rises JULIA comes out of the kitchen, humming to herself. She is a transformation. She wears an alluring evening dress, her hair is down, and her spectacles gone. She has a glass in one hand and a bottle of champagne in the other, and is already a little tipsy. She tops up her glass, puts the bottle into an ice bucket on the bar, and takes a swig. Looks round the room, checks the table, chuckles to herself, and turns the lights lower. Then turns, trips slightly, and goes a touch unsteadily back into the kitchen. A key rattles in the flat-door lock, the door opens, and DRAKE dashes in breathless. He glances at his watch, and peels off his jacket. He doesn't notice the table.)

DRAKE. *(Calling to kitchen.)* Hi, Jim! *(Loud crash of plates from kitchen)* Well done, mate! The show was sensational tonight. Did you watch it? *(Hangs his jacket in the wardrobe and continues talking.)* This is it, Jim. Tonight's the night! My sanity saved by Honey Tooks. She doesn't know it but she's going to be doing the best P.R. job of her life. *(Pours himself a vodka, still talking. Addresses the glass.)* Make me a God! *(Calls.)* Fate is on my side this time. I can feel it in my bones. *(He starts to take his trousers off as JULIA enters from kitchen behind him and poses seductively in the doorway.)* I don't care what happens. Nothing's going to stop me. Fire — flood — earthquake…!

JULIA. Sounds like a rough night. *(DRAKE freezes, then turns,*

his trousers somewhere round his knees. JULIA smiles charmingly.)
Why are you taking your trousers off? Are we going to have to swim
for it?

DRAKE. *(Bewildered.)* Julia? *(Peers.)* Is that you?

JULIA. *(In a femme fatale voice.)* It's the *new* Julia.

DRAKE. Pardon?

JULIA. Don't go away. I've been liberated.

(She goes back towards kitchen.)

DRAKE. *(Pulling himself together.)* Just a minute! *(She returns.)*
What are you doing here at this hour?

JULIA. Cooking your dinner.

DRAKE. Why?

JULIA. You're in need of care and attention.

DRAKE. Am I?

JULIA. And I'm the girl to give it to you. *(Sexily.)* Shall I tell you
what I've got in the oven?

DRAKE. In the, er...?

JULIA. My speciality. *(Huskily.)* Duck a l'orange.

(She poses seductively at the door and then goes.)

DRAKE. *(Pulling himself together again.)* Just a minute! *(JULIA
immediately returns and poses again.)* Look, just what are you...? I
didn't ask you to.... You've never before.... You look wonderful.

JULIA. Thank you. *(Indicates his trousers.)* I wish I could say the
same for you. Either pull 'em up or drop 'em.

DRAKE. *(Hastily doing up his trousers.)* Why have you suddenly
become so concerned for my welfare?

JULIA. *(Coming to him.)* PR.

DRAKE. P.R.? That's Honey's job.

JULIA. She's public. I'm private.

DRAKE. I see.

JULIA. We spend most of our time being nasty to each other. I
decided it was time for some reverse tactics. *(Puts her arms round his
neck, her glass still in one hand.)* After all, this is much pleasanter,

isn't it?

DRAKE. Much. As long as you don't spill that drink down the back of my neck.

JULIA. *(Drawing back.)* It's nearly empty. It needs filling up. *(She picks up the champagne bottle and pours.)* I found this in the fridge — I hope you don't mind.

DRAKE. Help yourself. *(Looking at watch.)* I, er....

JULIA. What was all that stuff about fire, floods and earthquakes?

DRAKE. Mm? Oh ... it's an idea for a film I might be doing.

JULIA. Wonderful. What's it called?

DRAKE. "Carry on Moses". Julia, how long are you, er ... going to be here?

JULIA. *(Pointedly.)* Why, have you got anything better to do?

DRAKE. No, no....

JULIA. *(Sweetly.)* Good.

(She starts to turn.)

DRAKE. That is ... *(She turns back.)* I'm supposed to be popping out for a bit.

JULIA. A bit of what?

DRAKE. A bit of, er ... business.

JULIA. Business?

DRAKE. Business. It means an awful lot to me if I can pull it.... Pull it off.

JULIA. *(Coming very close.)* You don't usually put business before pleasure. And I might never be ... available again. Think about it while I orange the duck.

(Buries her nose in her glass, and heads unsteadily back to the kitchen. As she goes she pushes two buttons on the panel. The lights lower and soft music is heard. DRAKE stands dazed for a moment, then gulps at his drink and takes a bewildered turn round the room.)

DRAKE. She's on ecstasy. What's happening? Suddenly I've got half London to choose from. *(To the ceiling.)* Are you playing games with me, fate?

(JULIA returns with two plates.)

JULIA. Here we are — first course. *(Wafts them seductively under his nose.)* Liver paté, lover boy.
DRAKE. I didn't know you could cook.
JULIA. There's a lot you don't know about me.
DRAKE. What about James?
JULIA. James is … out for the evening.
DRAKE. Doing what?

(JULIA giggles, then controls herself.)

JULIA. Business. *(Dances a few steps towards him.)* May I have this dance please.

(She puts her arms round his neck, and dances with him. Wraps herself progressively closer round him.)

DRAKE. *(Hoarse.)* Julia?
JULIA. Yes, darling?
DRAKE. What's the game?
JULIA. Game?
DRAKE. If you want a raise you don't have to go to all this trouble.
JULIA. Don't I?
DRAKE. Just ask.
JULIA. Can I have a raise?
DRAKE. No.
JULIA. So much for that.

(DRAKE, still dancing, looks at his watch behind her back. She starts to caress the back of his neck.)

DRAKE. I've never seen this side of you before.

JULIA. Do you like it?

DRAKE. Oh, yes, it's, um.... Look — about my business.

JULIA. *(Breaking away petulantly.)* I thought you'd forgotten that stupid 'business'.

DRAKE. I'd love to, but I don't see how I can. However, I've got an idea.

JULIA. What?

DRAKE. Why don't I nip off and attend to it now ... it shouldn't take too long — maybe an hour or so ... while you keep the dinner warm and watch telly, and drink some more champagne. Then when I get back we can carry on from where we are now.

JULIA. Watch telly?

DRAKE. Yes.

JULIA. While you ....

DRAKE. Do my business. What do you think?

(There is a pause.)

JULIA. I think I'll go and cut my throat.

(She storms into the kitchen. The door slams. He stares at it for a long moment.)

DRAKE. *(Bewildered.)* What did I say? Perfectly innocent remark.... *(Claps his hand to his head.)* She knows! She knows about Honey. Fool! Well that's that. Yet another cock-up. Still, it was a bit over-ambitious. Two at once on your first shot. *(Looks to heaven.)* You're still cooking 'em up, aren't you? *(He hesitates, then goes to the kitchen door.)* I'm sorry, Julia. It was an awful thing to suggest — even if you hadn't known. *(Pause.)* Julia? *(Pause.)* Please don't cut your throat. *(Tries the handle. It's locked.)* Julia, will you come out of there! What are you doing? *(Pause. Still no sound from the kitchen. He pulls himself together.)* Very well, if that's the way you want it. Stay there. Stay there all night. It was all your fault, anyway. I'm off to Honey's. *(Goes to the flat door.)* Good night.

(He slams the door, staying on the inside. JULIA flings open the

kitchen door, a bread knife in one hand.)

JULIA. No, Drake, please don't ... *(Tails off as she sees him.)* ... go.

DRAKE. *(Staring at the bread knife)* What's that for?

JULIA. To cut my throat with.

DRAKE. A bread knife?

JULIA. I felt like serrated edges.

DRAKE. *(Shuddering.)* Ugh! *(Awkwardly.)* I'm sorry. I'm very, very sorry.

JULIA. Rather optimistic time schedule, don't you think? There and back and ... everything in an hour?

DRAKE. *(Weakly.)* I could have kept the taxi waiting.

JULIA. I suppose I wasn't very subtle about it.

DRAKE. Oh, you had me on toast. You weren't to know I'd try and spread myself over two slices. *(Gently.)* Were you ... prepared for the consequences?

JULIA. *(Sitting, in a small voice.)* I thought, in for a penny, in for a pound.

DRAKE. *(Sincere.)* That's the best pound's worth I've ever been offered.

(He hesitates and then kneels beside her to kiss her. She almost succumbs, but pulls away at the last moment.)

JULIA. Hold on.

DRAKE. *(Falling into her lap.)* What is it?

JULIA. What about Honey Tooks? She's waiting for you.

DRAKE. I'll phone her. Tell her I can't make it.

(He dashes to the phone.)

JULIA. You needn't bother.

DRAKE. *(Stopping.)* Why not?

JULIA. She already knows.

DRAKE. She what?

JULIA. James is there now.

DRAKE. *(Bemused.)* James is?

JULIA. Explaining to her.

DRAKE. What about?

JULIA. This important business you had to do at home.

DRAKE. *(Comprehending.)* I see! *(Pause.)* You've thought of everything.

JULIA. Always the perfect secretary.

DRAKE. *(Coming back to kiss her.)* Perfect.

JULIA. Hold on!

(He again falls into her lap.)

DRAKE. What's the matter?

JULIA. Isn't there a certain protocol to observe?

DRAKE. Protocol?

JULIA. I mean you don't usually seduce a girl before the hors d'oeuvre, do you?

DRAKE. Not usually, no.

JULIA. *(Softening)* Although you're the expert.

DRAKE. Yes. *(Goes to kiss her, but stops again.)* Have, er … have you ever been seduced before the hors d'oeuvre?

JULIA. Not recently, no.

DRAKE. Well, perhaps we ought to stick to routine…

JULIA. *(Very close.)* You mean have supper first?

DRAKE. Well, perhaps the hors d'oeuvre….

JULIA. The duck could wait….

DRAKE. We could have the sweet later….

JULIA. There's plenty of time, isn't there?

DRAKE. But perhaps….

JULIA. What?

DRAKE. Just one kiss first?

JULIA. Just one. *(They go to kiss. She stops.)* Promise?

DRAKE. I promise.

(They slowly kiss. The kiss gets more passionate. Finally DRAKE breaks away, hurries to the settee and wades into his liver paté. JULIA is left frozen in her kissing position oblivious to the fact that

DRAKE has gone. After a moment she wakes up and realizes.)

JULIA. *(In a small voice.)* You beast!
DRAKE. What's the matter?
JULIA. How could you leave me in midair like that?
DRAKE. Just one kiss, you said. You made me promise.
JULIA. That's beside the point!
DRAKE. You said after the paté and before the duck.
JULIA. Did I? You start with the paté, I'll turn down the duck. *(She hurries towards kitchen but stops and turns.)* To hell with the duck!

(She grabs him from behind the settee and kisses him passionately. Rolls over on top of him. Eventually the embrace breaks, and DRAKE ends up on the floor.)

DRAKE. *(Weakly)* Bloody hell!
JULIA. *(Trembling)* I think we'd better have the paté first.

(They both start, trembling with excitement. DRAKE stops before the first mouthful.)

DRAKE. The hell with this! Turn down the duck.
JULIA. Right! *(JULIA gets up and rushes into the kitchen. DRAKE dashes to the control panel. He presses the bed button, and as the bed swings down hurries back to the settee. Reclines innocently as JULIA rushes back in.)* Shall I bring down the, er.... *(Turns to the bed and sees it is down.)* Ah. You've done it.
DRAKE. *(Rising.)* Yes.
JULIA. *(Losing courage.)* Jolly good. What do we do next?
DRAKE. I ... I take off your clothes.
JULIA. What about yours?
DRAKE. They come next.
JULIA. Right.
DRAKE. *(Going to her.)* Let me, er ....

(He tugs at the zipper of her dress. It's stuck.)

JULIA. Let me help.

(She frees the zipper. He rips the dress off her, picks her up in a most ungainly fashion and rushes with her to the bed. They fall onto it in a frantic embrace.)

JULIA. *(Suddenly sitting up.)* I'd better tell you!
DRAKE. *(Sitting up breathless.)* What?
JULIA. I've got to say it.
DRAKE. Never mind saying it, just let's do it!

(He pushes her back on the bed, kisses her, but again she sits up.)

JULIA. No! I haven't ... I haven't ....
DRAKE. Haven't what?
JULIA. Taken my pill.
DRAKE. Have you got a headache already?
JULIA. No! You know....
DRAKE. Oh.
JULIA. It's in my bag in the kitchen.
DRAKE. I'll get it! *(He rushes into the kitchen. JULIA gets off the bed, pushes the button on the panel and urges the bed back into the wall. DRAKE rushes back in from the kitchen with the pills.)* Voila! *(Dives onto where the bed ought to be. Crashes to the floor and rolls half across the room. Pause. Eventually, half dazed.)* What happened to the bed?
JULIA. I've changed my mind.
DRAKE. Why?!
JULIA. I'm not in the mood.

(He gets to his feet and goes towards her.)

DRAKE. Yes, you are.
JULIA. No, I'm not.
DRAKE. *(Grabbing her hands.)* You are.
JULIA. I'm not.
DRAKE. *(Fighting with her.)* Well *I* am!

JULIA. Well I'm *not*!! *(She pulls sharply away from him. He goes backwards towards the bed as she falls back onto the control panel. The bed comes down on his head [shoulders] with a great thump, he staggers downstage, and collapses unconscious over the settee. JULIA stands transfixed. Eventually she comes dazedly towards him. In a small voice.)* Drake. *(No response.)* Drake.

(She sinks weakly onto her knees in the middle of the floor and stares at the inert body. A few moments pass, then there is a knock on the door, and JAMES's voice calls tentatively.)

JAMES. Drake? Julia? Can I come in?

(Another knock)

JULIA. *(Softly.)* Come in.

(There is the rattle of a key in the lock, and he flings open the door, and stands there breathless. He sports a healthy black eye.)

JAMES. What's this — a seance?
JULIA. He's only unconscious.
JAMES. Oh, that *is* good news!

(JAMES closes the door and comes to look at DRAKE.)

JULIA. What happened to your eye?
JAMES. A bottle of Chanel Number 5.
JULIA. She threw it?
JAMES. Among other things.
JULIA. What happened?
JAMES. I simply said that Drake had some business and I'd come as a substitute. She said she was insulted, and then followed insult with injury. *(JULIA starts to cry.)* What are you crying for?
JULIA. I can't do anything right.
JAMES. I dunno. Two men out in one round can't be bad. What happened here?

JULIA. I knocked him out.

JAMES. What with?

JULIA. *(Wailing.)* The bed!

JAMES. *(Bemused.)* Why?

JULIA. I panicked.

JAMES. Well it's the first time I've heard of a girl using the actual bed to defend herself with.

JULIA. I thought sex was supposed to be simple!

JAMES. So did I, sweetheart!

JULIA. I should have gone through with it! I should have gone through with it!

JAMES. You got halfway by the look of you.

JULIA. *(Remembering her half undressed state.)* Oh.

(Goes to put on her dress again.)

JAMES. Why are you so desperate about it?

JULIA. Because I'm twenty-three.

JAMES. Is that a special year?

JULIA. I thought it was high time I did it. Everyone else is at it left, right and center.

JAMES. I dunno. Once upon a time chastity was an honor, a virtue. Now it's a social stigma, like halitosis! *(To DRAKE, slapping his cheek.)* Come on, sleeping prince.

(DRAKE groans but doesn't wake. JAMES takes ice from the ice bucket and puts it down DRAKE's trousers. DRAKE yells and leaps up. Shakes the ice down his trouser leg. He sees JULIA and gets behind JAMES for protection. Does a double-take on JAMES's eye.)

DRAKE. Got you as well, did she?

JAMES. That was Honey.

DRAKE. Serves you right.

JAMES. Thank you.

DRAKE. And don't try anything with this one. Her choice of weapon is most unusual.

JULIA. I'm so sorry, Draycott, darling. I pushed the wrong button.

DRAKE. You mean you meant to hit me with the wardrobe? *(He picks up his jacket and staggers to the door.)* Well, if you'll excuse me I'll just crawl round to Honey's place.

JULIA. *(Pleading.)* It was an accident!

DRAKE. Thank God you weren't trying!

(He exits and JULIA goes into a flood of tears. JAMES looks uncomfortable.)

JAMES. The human body is only seven-tenths water, you know. If you cry any more today you'll collapse in a pile of dust.

(The entry phone buzzer goes and JULIA hurries to it.)

JULIA. Draycott! *(Speaking into the intercom.)* Forgive me, darling.

HONEY. *(Voice over.)* We'll see about that!

JAMES. *(Looking around for cover.)* God, it's her!

JULIA. *(To JAMES.)* She must have missed Drake.

JAMES. *(Feeling his eye.)* She doesn't miss very often.

JULIA. *(Into intercom.)* Draycott isn't here, Honey.

HONEY. Press that thing or I'll break the door down.

JULIA. *(Into intercom.)* Alright, alright.

(She presses the button.)

JAMES. No! What did you do that for?

JULIA. You heard her.

JAMES. *(Heading for the spare room.)* Tell her I've gone back to Australia.

JULIA. It's Draycott she's after.

JAMES. He's welcome to her!

(He exits into spare room. JULIA hesitates and then presses the button to bring the desk into position. She puts the flat door on the latch,

takes the candelabra from the table, puts it on the desk and sits down, typing at the typewriter. HONEY comes in the flat door, wearing another provocative outfit. She surveys the scene and then walks down to behind JULIA who is still typing ostentatiously.)

HONEY. Who are you supposed to be? Liberace?

JULIA. Oh. Good evening, Honey. You've caught me doing some overtime.

HONEY. No comment. *(Surveys JULIA.)* Smart office outfit, but your zipper's undone.

(Zips it up for her.)

JULIA. Thank you.

HONEY. Yes, you've smartened up in more ways than one. Where's Draycott?

JULIA. Gone round to your place.

HONEY. You don't say? Finished his 'business' here then, did he?

JULIA. Almost.

HONEY. I see. And James is in the spare room, is he?

JULIA. How did you know?

HONEY. I can scent a man at a hundred yards range, sweetie. So … you worked out a neat little scheme tonight, didn't you?

JULIA. I'm very sorry, Honey.

HONEY. What exactly was the idea?

JULIA. To seduce Draycott before you did.

HONEY. And it didn't work out?

JULIA. I used the wrong side of the bed.

HONEY. Oh. *(Frowns.)* Eh?

JULIA. I hit him on the head with it.

HONEY. Using your subtle technique, were you?

JULIA. I've just never seduced anybody before.

HONEY. Quite right. Our job is to get them to seduce us.

JULIA. I've never done that either.

(Pause.)

HONEY. When you say never done it ...?

JULIA. I mean never done it.

HONEY. You mean you're a ...

JULIA. Virgin!

HONEY. Phew!! I thought they were extinct. How long have you *been* a vir... sorry, that's a silly question isn't it? I'm beginning to see now. You're in love with Draycott. I thought you just fancied him.

JULIA. I don't think I know the difference.

HONEY. Well no wonder you haven't made first base yet! *(Holds out a key.)* Look, here's the key to my flat. It's round the corner — 34 George Street — if you hurry you'll catch him.

JULIA. I can't go after him again. He thinks I'm just a tease!

HONEY. Well don't play so hard to get this time. Dinner's in the oven, drinks are in the cupboard, and you use the side of the bed facing the ceiling.

JULIA. But, I ....

HONEY. No buts. Go!

(She pushes JULIA out of the door. Closes it and looks towards the spare room. She deliberately slams the front door and hides against the wall. JAMES immediately comes out of the spare room.)

JAMES. Has she gone?

HONEY. Yes.

JAMES. *(Seeing HONEY.)* Oh God! Where's Julia?

HONEY. I sent her after Drake.

JAMES. I thought *you* wanted him.

HONEY. Ah, but she loves him. There's a difference.

JAMES. Yes, well....

HONEY. *(Seeing his eye.)* Oh, your poor eye. Did I do that?

JAMES. It's all right, I've got another one.

HONEY. I'm sorry, but palming me off with a substitute is no way to treat a girl.

JAMES. Look that substitute business wasn't really my idea.

HONEY. I suspected that. You're not the hunting sort — more the prey.

JAMES. *(Uneasily.)* You could say that, yes.

HONEY. I'm the other way round.

JAMES. I've noticed.

HONEY. What's the matter? You seem nervous.

JAMES. Just a little.

HONEY. We've got it right now. I've come to you.

JAMES. That's what makes me nervous.

HONEY. You're rather sweet, James. I like shy men.

JAMES. *(Resigned.)* Here we go again.

HONEY. Let's make ourselves at home. I wonder what's for dinner.

JAMES. I don't know — no-one's managed to get that far yet.

HONEY. *(Going towards the kitchen.)* Smells good. *(As she opens kitchen door and peers in, JAMES tiptoes to the front door.)* Duck! *(JAMES takes her literally and drops to the ground. She looks round. He foolishly rises again.)* I like a nice dinner afterwards.

JAMES. *(Warily.)* Afterwards?

HONEY. Is that champagne I see there?

JAMES. Er, yes. I could do with a drink myself.

(He pours her champagne, and whiskey for himself. As he does so she turns the lights lower, which makes JAMES look up nervously.)

HONEY. That's cozier.

JAMES. I can hear you, but I can't quite see you.

HONEY. Here.

(She sits on the settee. He hands her the glass from a distance, and picks up a bowl of nuts.)

JAMES. Nut?

HONEY. Lovely. *(JAMES, keeping his distance from her, tosses her a nut.)* That's not very gentlemanly. Come and sit next to me.

JAMES. No thanks. *(Indicates his eye.)* You're rather dangerous at short range.

HONEY. I want to make amends for that.

JAMES. I've forgiven you.

HONEY. But I haven't. I want to be friends again.
JAMES. We are.
HONEY. Then come and make love to me.

(JAMES is in the act of squirting soda into his whiskey. The shock of her remark shoots it way over his glass.)

JAMES. Good Lord! Don't you think there should be some pre-liminaries?

(HONEY stands and sings.)

HONEY. 'God Save Our Gracious Queen....'
JAMES. Belt up! This isn't a sporting event!
HONEY. What do you want from a woman, James?
JAMES. Peace and quiet!
HONEY. We don't have to make a lot of noise about it.
JAMES. A bit of *grace*.
HONEY. *(Praying.)* For what we are about to receive ....
JAMES. *(In despair.)* What I'm trying to say is ....
HONEY. That you don't find me desirable.
JAMES. *(With a sigh.)* Oh, on the contrary, I find you highly de-sirable. That's my trouble — I find *all* desirable women desirable. When one like you turns up, I begin to fear for my soul.
HONEY. It's not your soul I want.
JAMES. I know that!
HONEY. Oh, what a lovely man you are! Come here.
JAMES. *(Retreating.)* I think someone should see how the din-ner's doing. Something may be overcooking in there.
HONEY. I don't think so.
JAMES. Well, it is in here!

(He hurries into the kitchen. HONEY looks thoughtfully around, then goes to the control panel. She cautiously inspects the buttons.)

HONEY. Eeny, meeny, miny, mo.... *(Presses a button and the bed descends.)* Bull's eye! (*She climbs onto the bed and reclines*

there, leaning against the backrest. Calling.) James. *(Pause.)* James!
You can't stay there all night.
    JAMES. *(Off.)* You want to bet?
    HONEY. You can't sleep on the draining-board.
    JAMES. *(Off.)* You want to bet?
    HONEY. Well then, I'll just have to come in there and seduce
you on it.
    JAMES. *(Off.)* You wouldn't dare!
    HONEY. You want to bet?!

*(The kitchen door opens, and JAMES comes out. He has a pan lid in
one hand as a shield, and a potato masher in the other, at the
ready. He peers round the room for HONEY. Sees her.)*

    JAMES. *(Sighing hopelessly.)* Oh God!
    HONEY. *(Laughing.)* You can't fight me off with a potato-
masher.
    JAMES. *(Raising it.)* You just try me!
    HONEY. Oh, no, darling. I don't believe in violence. I've got
much subtler methods.
    JAMES. Such as? *(She seductively undoes a couple of buttons on
her dress, then sprawls out tantalizingly on the bed. JAMES blanches
and swallows hard.)* Leaves me cold. *(She stands up on the bed, undoes the rest of the buttons. He shakes his head.)* Leaves me cold.
*(She slips off the dress, drops it delicately on one side, and stands
there in her bra and pants. He is shaking so much that the potato-
masher is rattling against the pan lid. She puts a hand on her bra
strap.)* Hold it!!
    HONEY. You're cracking.
    JAMES. I am not cracking!
    HONEY. Come here then.
    JAMES. I won't come there!
    HONEY. I shall go on taking things off until you do.
    JAMES. You haven't got much more to take off!
    HONEY. You've got five seconds.
    JAMES. I've never met such a female in my life!
    HONEY. *(Beaming.)* And you probably won't again so take ad-

vantage of it. *(Slips one bra strap off her shoulder.)* Four.
JAMES. You can't bully me like that.
HONEY. *(Removing the other strap.)* Three.
JAMES. I don't give in to blackmail.
HONEY. *(Undoing the clasp.)* Two.
JAMES. I'm warning you...!
HONEY. One .

(She is now holding the undone bra to her front.)

JAMES. Zero! *(JAMES leaps forward to the control panel, and presses the button. The bed goes up just a she drops the bra, and HONEY disappears into the wall with a squeal, the bra flying up and into the room. He calls through the bed, triumphant.)* How was that for 'lift off'?

(He exits into the kitchen. A moment passes, then the bed shakes, and comes away from the wall a few inches. It goes back, comes out, goes back and finally an arm manages to squeeze out and feel up and down the wall for the control panel. It finds a button, presses, and the bed descends with HONEY on board wrapped in the bedcover. She lies there for a moment, recovering her composure.)

HONEY. That, I suppose, is what they call sending one up the wall. *(She climbs unsteadily off the bed, and looks towards the kitchen.)* Very well, if he wants to play it rough....

(She presses the button, and sends the bed back into the wall. She nips across to the other side of the kitchen door and flattens herself against the wall. JAMES comes out, carrying a bottle of wine. He glances at the bed.)

JAMES. *(Calling.)* Let me know when the oxygen's running out — I'll bore a hole.
HONEY. *(Behind him.)* Thank you.
JAMES. *(Calling.)* Pleasure. *(He sees her and does a double-*

take.) Oh, no! How did you get out?

HONEY. There's very little I can't do with a bed, James. *(With an evil smile.)* So it's electronic warfare you want, is it?

JAMES. *(Backing away.)* Now just a minute.... *(She presses buttons and the wardrobe revolves with JAMES on it, as music comes blaring in and lights flash on and off. JAMES leaps off as she brings the bed in, which knocks him towards the desk, on which he revolves again, leaping off into the drinks cabinet, which knocks him under the TV as it descends, sending him diving onto the bed, which promptly goes up into the wall and back again, depositing him with a final crash flat on his face. He gasps.)* All right, I give in! I give in!

HONEY. *(Beaming.)* Wasn't that fun?

JAMES. *(Breathless.)* You're a maniac!

HONEY. You started it.

JAMES. Well, let's call it quits now, shall we?

HONEY. *(Dropping the bed cover and advancing.)* Oh, I never quit when I'm winning.

JAMES. *(Retreating.)* Oh no. You're outrageous!

HONEY. This is the age of 'Women's Lib,' James. We're allowed to do as much seducing as you are.

JAMES. This isn't seduction — it's rape!

HONEY. *(Backing him onto the bed.)* Don't be silly. How can a frail little woman like me rape a great big man like you?

(She arm wrestles him and forces him slowly back down on the bed.)

JAMES. I don't know, but it looks suspiciously as if I'm going to find out.

(As she falls on top of him the door opens and DRAKE enters, somewhat out of breath. They break. He stares, unable to believe his eyes.)

DRAKE. *(Furious.)* How does he *do* it??

HONEY. I was just about to find out.

DRAKE. I don't understand. I just don't understand what's going on.

HONEY. Drake darling, calm down.

DRAKE. Calm down! When I find you half naked, and my own brother seducing you on my bed?

HONEY. Don't be silly. I'm seducing him.

(She wraps herself in the bedcover.)

DRAKE. You're not fussy who you seduce, are you?

JAMES. *(Sweetly.)* Thank you very much!

HONEY. Believe it or not I'm *very* fussy.

DRAKE. Where's Julia?

HONEY. No, she's not my type.

DRAKE. Where *is* she? *(The phone rings. They all look at it. Nervous.)* Who do you suppose that is?

JAMES. Fate, mate.

HONEY. That'll be her.

DRAKE. Jim — answer it.

JAMES. She can't want me.

DRAKE. *(Beseechingly.)* Honey.

HONEY. Nor me, darling.

(DRAKE hesitatingly answers the phone.)

DRAKE. *(Imitating MRS. FINNEY.)* Hello, Mrs. Finney speaking.... Who ...? *(Normal voice.)* Oh, it's you Mrs. Finney. Sorry. Mr. Finney? No, he's not up here.... He went to the pub at lunchtime, and you haven't seen him since? Well I shouldn't worry. Short of searching every pub in London, I can't suggest .... *(Stops thoughtfully.)* Just a minute, have you put the kids to bed? Do you like duck a l'orange? Well, how about having some with me tonight?

JAMES. That's really going from the sublime to the ridiculous.

DRAKE. *(On phone.)* No, I'm not joking. I'm on my own tonight. A drop of wine, watch the telly....

HONEY. Hold hands.

DRAKE. *(On phone.)* Soon as you like. Come as you are. *(Replaces the receiver and turns to the others.)* There we are. You two can go and play games elsewhere. I'm opting out. *(He opens the flat door for them.)* And if you meet Julia on the way take her with you.

(He exits into kitchen.)

JAMES. *(To HONEY.)* Come on. *(Throws her dress to her.)* Get your clothes on.

HONEY. I'm not leaving Mrs. Finney to walk off with Draycott after all we've been through..

JAMES. Which one of us *are* you after, me or Drake?

HONEY. You'll find out. Now you go and find Julia and bring her back here. I'll stay and get rid of Mrs. Finney.

JAMES. How?

HONEY. I have my means.

(She drops the bed cover as she bends down to collect her bra. JAMES watches her behind.)

JAMES. I hope they're better hidden than your ends.

HONEY. Get Julia!

(She hurries into the bathroom with her clothes. He dashes after her.)

JAMES. Wait a minute! How do I ...? What am I supposed to ...?

(JAMES futilely rattles the door handle. DRAKE comes out of the kitchen and sees him.)

DRAKE. What are you doing?

JAMES. *(Awkwardly.)* I was just, er ... I just wanted a ... I can wait.

(JAMES goes towards the flat door.)

DRAKE. Fat lot of help you've been this evening. Whose side are you on anyway?

JAMES. *(Petulantly.)* No one's. I'm not playing anymore. *(Starts to go, and almost bumps into MRS. FINNEY as she appears in the doorway. She is dressed in party best with her hair exotically done and a feather boa. JAMES reacts.)* My God it's Naomi Campbell. *(Leads her down to a bemused DRAKE and puts their hands together.)* Till death do you part.

(JAMES hurries out of flat door. DRAKE retrieves his hand, and MRS. FINNEY poses about the room.)

MRS. F. *(Posh.)* What a charming place you have here.

DRAKE. Do sit down Mrs. Finney. What'll you have to drink?

MRS. F. I'll have a campari and soda, if I may.

DRAKE. I'm not sure if I've got any campari.

MRS. F. Bottom shelf. I think there's some left. *(Arranges herself on the settee.)* I can't imagine what's happened to my old man. With any luck he's emigrated. *(As he starts to pour her drink.)* To the top please ... with the campari, not the soda. Well, this is a turn up for the book isn't it? You having to resort to me.

DRAKE. Not at all. I thought it was a good opportunity to cement our relationship.

MRS. F. *(Suspiciously.)* To what?

DRAKE. To get to know each other a bit better.

MRS. F. Oh, yes.

DRAKE. Excuse me. I'll just see to the duck.

MRS. F. Of course, you know, I am the envy of all my friends.

DRAKE. Why?

MRS. F. Well ... looking after Draycott Harris.

DRAKE. *(Flattered.)* Oh, I see.

MRS. F. Mind you, I don't tell them it's like working in a kindergarten, a refugee camp and a brothel rolled into one.

DRAKE. Thank you.

(He exits to the kitchen. MRS. FINNEY poses grandly on the settee, and has some fun with her drink and her feather boa.)

MRS. F. *(Singing.)* Who wants to be a millionaire ...?

(HONEY enters wearing an exotic dressing gown over her bra and pants. She is wearing sun glasses and smoking a cigarette. She is also wearing large colorful bed socks. MRS. FINNEY stares.)

HONEY. *(Singing)* "Fly me to the moon ..." *(Sees MRS. FINNEY)* Oh, hello.

MRS. F. What are you doing here? *(HONEY removes her sunglasses and lets the dressing gown fall open. MRS. FINNEY reacts in shock.)* Where's your frock?

HONEY. Who needs frocks? Have you come to join in?

MRS. F. Join in what?

HONEY. The party.

MRS. F. Party? It's just Mr. Harris and me.

HONEY. Don't be silly. How can two people have an orgy?

MRS. F. Orgy!?

HONEY. I never realized you went in for this sort of thing, Mrs. Finney.

MRS. F. I don't. I'm only here for the duck.

HONEY. Oh, well you are in for a surprise. You can be in the middle.

MRS. F. Middle! *(She rises angrily.)* I thought it was a bit odd, all that stuff about putting cement on my relations. I only came up because my old man has vanished.

HONEY. I expect he's coming too. Come on Mrs. Finney, I'll let the bed down and we can try it out.

(She lets the bed down, throws off her dressing gown, and bounces enthusiastically on the mattress.)

MRS. F. No thank you! I'm going.

HONEY. Don't go. It'll be an experience.

MRS. F. Experience! Listen deary, I've had more experience than you've had hot showers. You should have been around during the sixties. *(At the door.)* I've only three words to say to you — Rolling Stone concerts!

(MRS. FINNEY exits angrily. HONEY bends down to take the bed

socks off as DRAKE enters and gets her rear view.)

DRAKE. Mrs. Finney?
HONEY. *(Straightening.)* Hello darling.
DRAKE. Honey! What the hell are you doing here?
HONEY. Don't worry. I'm not staying.
DRAKE. Where's Mrs. Finney?
HONEY. She's decided it's too hot for her here. James is sending Julia back. *(Hands him the bed socks and the dressing gown.)* You can have these back now.

(HONEY goes into the bathroom to get her dress.)

DRAKE. I don't want Julia back.

(She returns with the dress and starts to put it on.)

HONEY. Of course you do.
DRAKE. I don't.
HONEY. You do. Zip me up.

(As he does so, the flat door opens and JULIA enters. She stops on seeing the pair of them in a compromising position.)

JULIA. Ooooh!
DRAKE. Where's the bread knife?

(He hurries into kitchen.)

JULIA. So that's what James meant when he said I'd find a surprise waiting for me!
HONEY. Don't be ridiculous. *(Searches).* Where's my shoe. It's the other half of this foolish family I'm interested in.
JULIA. James?
HONEY. *(Putting on her shoes.)* Of course.
JULIA. *(Indicating the kitchen.)* It's this fool you've been chasing.

HONEY. Well, it's that fool I'm after. Now, I'm leaving you to make a fool of yourself with this fool. *(Wags a finger.)* But don't fool yourself. He's a fool!

JULIA. I can't.

HONEY. Why? You've got nothing to worry about.

JULIA. I have.

HONEY. Relax. Just look upon it like losing your baby teeth.

JULIA. That wasn't very enjoyable.

HONEY. No, but it was inevitable, and left you much better equipped for future dinners.

(She blows a kiss and exits. JULIA plucks up her courage and goes to the kitchen door.)

JULIA. *(Calls through the door.)* Mr. Harris? *(Knocks.)* Mr. Harris?

DRAKE. *(Off.)* What is it?

JULIA. Will you come and make love to me, please?

(There is a thunderous crash of pots and pans off-stage.)

CURTAIN

SCENE 2

(The next morning. The curtains are open, and sunshine streams into the room. JULIA lies asleep in the bed. The flat door opens, and MRS. FINNEY enters wearing hat and coat and carrying a shopping bag. She goes to the bed and looks down at the sleeping JULIA.)

MRS. F. Poor Julia. Another sacrifice on the altar of erotic dreams.

(DRAKE enters from bathroom in the dressing gown HONEY used the night before.)

DRAKE. Good morning, Mrs. Finney.
MRS. F. Huh!

(She exits smartly to the kitchen. DRAKE follows to the kitchen door.)

DRAKE. *(Through the door.)* I'm sorry about last night....

(She comes out of kitchen minus shopping bag, barging past him.)

MRS. F. Huh!

(MRS. FINNY exits bathroom, taking off hat and coat. He follows to the door.)

DRAKE. Look, will you let me explain?

(She marches out minus hat and coat.)

MRS. F. Huh!
DRAKE. Mrs. Finney — is this going to go on all morning?
MRS. F. *(Turning.)* I hope you enjoyed yourselves last night.

DRAKE. Please, let me explain!

MRS. F. *(Aloof.)* I do not need an explanation. *(Looks at JULIA.)* I only hope Julia didn't get more than she bargained for.

DRAKE. Julia....

MRS. F. You certainly look as if *you* did.

DRAKE. Like everyone else, I spent a very chaotic evening last night, due mostly to you and your advice.

MRS. F. Well, anyway, if I were you I'd see to your brother. He looks as if no one's told him it's over yet.

DRAKE. James? Where is he?

MRS. F. On his way up, if he can find the lift. I passed him trying to get the broom cupboard off the ground.

(She exits to the kitchen. DRAKE goes to the flat door, opens it, and recoils as JAMES enters with his key at the ready. He looks even worse for wear than DRAKE. He yawns copiously as he walks in a trance to the settee and sits.)

JAMES. 'Morning.

DRAKE. You look as if you've had a hard night.

JAMES. I have. I spent it in Honey's bath.

DRAKE. As long as it wasn't full.

JAMES. It nearly was by morning. The cold tap dripped.

DRAKE. What was wrong with her bed?

JAMES. She was in it. The only way to escape her was to lock myself in the bathroom. Besides, it can't have been a very good bed.

DRAKE. Why not?

JAMES. She spent half the night trying to join me in the bath! In the end she broke the door in. I had to fight her off with my loofa. She's got a surplus of hormones that girl. I got away smartly this morning, before she woke up, had a plate of porridge and started off again. *(Sees the table, still laid for dinner the evening before.)* Oh good — liver paté for breakfast!

(JAMES sits and starts eating toast and paté with gusto.)

DRAKE. Be my guest.

JAMES. *(Indicating JULIA.)* Who's that in the bed?

DRAKE. Julia.

JAMES. So you finally got there. Congratulations.

DRAKE. *(Flatly.)* Got where? I spent the night on the kitchen draining board.

JAMES. Well, if that's how she gets her kicks....

DRAKE. She spent it there.

(He points to the bed)

JAMES. *(Indicating the kitchen.)* And you spent it in there?

DRAKE. *(Nodding.)* You should try sleeping on a draining board some time. I've got a corrugated back.

JAMES. I don't believe it! Were you too much of a coward to come and join her?

DRAKE. I would have done if I could have got out of the kitchen. She locked me in!

JAMES. *(Shaking his head.)* Strange girl, that one.

DRAKE. She didn't let me out until half an hour ago.

JAMES. Why then?

DRAKE. I was threatening to pee in the sink.

JAMES. Ah. *(Holds up the champagne bottle.)* Glass of champagne?

DRAKE. No thanks. *(JAMES pours himself a glass and drinks.)* She's a head case. She came all the way back last night specially to go to bed with me — then just when I'm on the boil and raring to go she sends me into the kitchen for a glass of water.

JAMES. She must have thought it was going to be thirsty work.

DRAKE. I don't know what she was thinking. All I know is I got her the glass of water and then found myself locked in!

JAMES. Did she say anything?

DRAKE. Not a word. I was livid, I can tell you. I hammered on the door, I shouted at her to open it, and all she did was burst into tears!

JAMES. Oh, lord. I get the picture. I bet you went at her like a bull at a gate.

DRAKE. Well I was worked up, of course I was. That was her

doing. But you don't get a bloke all raring to go and then lock him up in the kitchen.

JAMES. Poor Julia.

DRAKE. Poor *Julia?*

JAMES. She obviously hasn't told you.

DRAKE. Told me what?

JAMES. My God, the way everyone tries to hide it round here you'd think it came under the Official Secrets Act!

DRAKE. What?

JAMES. Julia's got the same problem you have.

DRAKE. Slightly short-sighted?

JAMES. *(After a beat.)* That's one way of putting it. Actually I was referring to your *other* problem. She's never done it before either.

DRAKE. Done what?

JAMES. Oh for God's sake!

DRAKE. *(Realizing.)* Julia?

JAMES. Yep.

DRAKE. You mean Julia's a .:.?

JAMES. Yep.

DRAKE. I don't believe it.

JAMES. Why not?

DRAKE. Well, I ... I thought I was the only one left.

JAMES. Well, you're not! So now you know. There are at least two of you on the planet. *(Wipes his mouth on a napkin.)* Ah, that was very nice. I won't stay for the liqueurs. If you'll excuse me I'll pop out and leave the pair of you to resolve the problem as best you can.

DRAKE. *(Urgently.)* No, Jim! You can't leave us alone together.

JAMES. Why not? Now you know what's been bothering the girl just treat her gently.

DRAKE. But can't you see — this is why we're so lethal for each other? It's the blind leading the blind.

JAMES. Well that'll save you putting the lights out then, won't it?

(He moves to go.)

DRAKE. *(Barring his way.)* Jim, please.

JAMES. *(In exasperation.)* For Heaven's sake, what's the matter with you? Look, this is love! Love!! The music that every man yearns for!

DRAKE. Not me — I don't know how to conduct!

JAMES. Just get your baton out and wave it around! You can't expect to be Toscanini in one go. Get together with her on the elementary scales and work up to the fifth symphony gradually.

(He pulls away again and tried to leave.)

DRAKE. You can't leave me, Jim!

JAMES. Well, I'm not stopping for the concert!

DRAKE. No, please, please....

JAMES. Let me go! *(They are almost wrestling by the flat door, when the intercom buzzer goes. JAMES reacts to its noise in his ear.)* God, the Albert Hall's got nothing on this place!

(DRAKE answers the entry phone.)

DRAKE. Hello?

HONEY. *(Voice over.)* 'Morning, darling. Let me in.

JAMES. *(Panic stricken)* It's her! I'm off!

DRAKE. Jim!

JAMES. Is there a fire escape from this place?

(He dashes about, round and over the bed with DRAKE in pursuit.)

DRAKE. Jim, no! Please! I can't cope with *both* of them. A virgin and a nymphomaniac!

JAMES. *(Still seeking a way out.)* Look, it's your problem, chum. You hired them.

DRAKE. You're my manager.

JAMES. I've resigned!

DRAKE. Jim!

(The buzzer goes again.)

JAMES. If we tied some sheets together could I make it out of the window?

(MRS. FINNEY enters from the kitchen.)

MRS. F. Isn't anyone going to answer that?
DRAKE. *(Trying to stop her.)* No!
MRS. F. *(To entry phone.)* Come up then.

(She presses buzzer.)

JAMES. Oh God!

(JAMES sprints for the bathroom and slams the door.)

DRAKE. *(To MRS. FINNEY.)* Now you've done it. That's Honey Tooks.
MRS. F. Are we starting all over again? *(JULIA sits up in bed. She is wearing one of Drake's pajama tops. She yawns.)* Good morning, Julia.
JULIA. Oh. Good morning, Mrs. Finney.
DRAKE. *(Gently.)* Good morning, Julia.
JULIA. *(Coldly.)* Good morning, Draycott.
MRS. F. Oh dear, back to square one. I thought you two were on each other.
DRAKE. Would you like to rephrase that?
MRS. F. *(To JULIA.)* Didn't it work out then, dear?
JULIA. Definitely not.
MRS. F. Ah well. What will be will be. Even if it never happens. Perhaps the ingredients weren't quite right...
DRAKE. Don't start your cookery lessons again, Mrs. Finney!
MRS. F. *(Haughty.)* Perhaps some of the ingredients are long past their sell-by date!

(She exits to the kitchen.)

JULIA. *(Getting out of bed.)* If you'll excuse me I'll get dressed.

(Indicates the bed.) Has everyone finished with this?

(DRAKE nods and JULIA presses button. The bed goes up. JULIA collects her clothes.)

DRAKE. Julia, I think we ought to have a talk.

(The bathroom door opens and JAMES comes out wearing MRS. FIN-NEY's hat and coat. He heads for the flat door.)

JAMES. *(Imitating MRS. FINNEY's voice.)* I'm off, Mr. Harris. See you later.
DRAKE. Fine.... *(Realizes.)* Hey!

(As JAMES makes a dash for the flat door MRS. FINNEY comes out from the kitchen in his path. She does a double-take on seeing JAMES in her clothes.)

MRS. F. Hey! My clothes!
JAMES. Oh God!

(She goes to grab him but JAMES evades her and dashes out of front door.)

MRS. F. *(Outraged.)* Well!!
JULIA. Excuse me.

(JULIA hurries into the spare room with her clothes. DRAKE goes to follow her, but the front door opens and JAMES dashes back in. He slams the door and leans against it, panting for breath.)

JAMES. Who let her in?? She was waiting for me outside the lift like a vampire!
MRS. F. You! Give me back my clothes!
JAMES. All right, all right!

(She pushes him round the room, ripping her coat and hat from him.)

MRS. F. *(At the kitchen door.)* I've heard about people like you!

(She storms out.)

DRAKE. Where's Honey now?
JAMES. Right behind me. Where can I go?

(He dashes to the spare room.)

DRAKE. No, not there...!
JULIA. *(Off.)* Hey!

(He shuts the door again hurriedly.)

JAMES. God, they're everywhere!

(JAMES dashes to the bathroom and slams the door. The flat doorbell rings. DRAKE collapses resignedly onto the sofa.)

MRS. F. *(Re-entering.)* You need a full-time doorman up here.

(She opens the door and HONEY marches in.)

HONEY. Where is he?
MRS. F. Gone.

(Without breaking her stride HONEY marches to the bathroom door and calls.)

HONEY. I'm waiting for you, James.
MRS. F. She's got built-in radar!
HONEY. *(Turning.)* Good morning, Mrs. Finney.
MRS. F. What's good about it?
HONEY. What's wrong? Still not got your husband back?
MRS. F. Oh yes, he's back. Three o'clock in the morning, dead broke and fighting drunk. Offered me a cold bag of fish and chips as if it was a bunch of roses.

HONEY. Why don't you leave him, for heaven's sake?

MRS. F. 'Cos I love him you fool!

(She exits emotionally in to kitchen.)

HONEY. Have you and Julia sorted yourselves out?

DRAKE. Julia and I don't need sorting out. Julia and I are having nothing further to do with each other.

HONEY. After all the trouble we took to get things back to normal.

DRAKE. There is nothing normal about my secretary.

HONEY. You must try and understand, Draycott, — poor Julia's got a bit of a ....

DRAKE. *(Cutting in.)* Problem! I know! Everybody seems to know. What's she done — put it in the hands of an advertising agent?

HONEY. Well, sex is a very difficult thing for some people.

DRAKE. You don't have to tell me. I'm one of them.

HONEY. Pardon?

DRAKE. I've got the same problem!

HONEY. What problem?

DRAKE. *The* problem! I've never done it! I've never had it! I'm never going to get it! I'll be the first virgin ever to collect his old age pension.

HONEY. *(Astounded.)* But you're the most renowned wolf in London.

DRAKE. I'm a sheep in wolf's clothing.

HONEY. Wow! A male virgin. It never occurred to me there was such a thing. I'd offer to help you out, my sweet, but I've got a bit of a problem myself.

DRAKE. Don't tell me you're one.

HONEY. How dare you! *(Thoughtfully.)* I don't think I ever was one. No, my problem is, I think I've fallen in love with James.

(DRAKE hesitates, then bursts out laughing.)

DRAKE. That'll make his day!

HONEY. *(Suddenly.)* I've got an idea!

DRAKE. *(Quickly.)* No, thank you.

HONEY. It could be the answer to all our problems. *(She goes to bathroom door and calls.)* James, come out of there. James! I want a word with you.

JAMES. *(Off.)* How many letters has it got?

HONEY. *(Imperatively.)* Come here!

(The door opens, and JAMES comes out. His face is covered in shaving cream, and he carries a safety razor threateningly.)

JAMES. Yep?

HONEY. You look like Santa Claus.

JAMES. This stuff has its uses. People think twice about assaulting you with this on your face.

HONEY. Listen — I've just learnt the cause of all our troubles. Drake and Julia are both in the same boat, as it were.

JAMES. So?

HONEY. Well, it seems to me that you and I aren't going to get ourselves sorted out until they are sorted out.

JAMES. We've nothing to sort out.

HONEY. 'Course we have, you silly man. Now — if you take Julia under your wing, and I take Drake under mine, then when they've learnt the basic rules of the game, we can all start again at the beginning. *(DRAKE whistles. JAMES stares open-mouthed.)* It's just a matter of the wolves helping the sheep over the stile.

JAMES. Now, listen here, little Bo-peep! If you mean what I think you mean, that's the most outrageous proposal I've ever heard in my life!

HONEY. Oh don't be silly! All I'm suggesting is ....

JAMES. *(Exploding.)* I don't care what you're suggesting, woman! Just leave me out of your blasted fertility rights!

HONEY. *(Taken aback.)* Oh.

(They stare at him, startled at his outburst.)

JAMES. *(Apoplectic with anger.)* I've had just about as much of this as I can stand! I warn you! I warn you — under this amiable, insignificant exterior lies a streak of violence that's about to explode any minute now! *(Calms a bit.)* I'm usually a mild sort of man as you know — an obliging sort of chap who'll do most things to help people.... *(Explodes again.)* But I've had enough fireworks this last twenty-four hours to last me a lifetime! I've been sent backwards and forward like some consolation prize in a lottery! I've been assaulted — physically, emotionally, and sexually! I've been wept on, stepped on, and practically slept on! I've been used as a pawn in everyone's game but my own, and I've had *enough* of it! *(Strides round the room.)* I've never met such a bunch in my life! I was under the naive impression that, having had a few experiences in odd parts of the globe, I knew a bit about the facts of life, but the way things move round here makes the Kama Sutra read like Winnie The Pooh! I always considered sex was merely a means of propagating the species. I thought its pleasures were just a by-product to keep the interest going. Here it seems to be a matter of life and death! *(The games room door opens quietly, and JULIA appears, unnoticed. She wears the same clothes as the night before.)* I get the impression I'm surrounded by a bunch of lust-crazed wild animals hounding each other through the jungle. One never knows from one moment to the next, whether one's going to get attacked, exterminated, or simply lassoed and sent out to stud! I don't know who frightens me most: Drake, who's suicidal because he's so far missed the boat; Honey, who's out to catch every boat that's going; or Mrs. Finney who seems to think she's the bloody harbor master! And as for Julia — she's the pick of the bunch! Julia ....

JULIA. Julia what?

JAMES. *(Turning.)* Oh God!

JULIA. You're right, James.

JAMES. Eh?

JULIA. But Julia's abandoning ship.

DRAKE. What does that mean?

JULIA. *(Quietly.)* I'm leaving you now — for good.

DRAKE. You can't do that!

JULIA. Why not?

DRAKE. I need you.

JULIA. No, you don't. You need a secretary with other skills beside shorthand and typing. There are plenty of them around.

DRAKE. I don't want them. I want you.

JULIA. Exactly. You want me — just as you want all the others. You were in such a rush last night, I thought you had a bus to catch or something! *(DRAKE looks abashed at JAMES, who gestures back hopelessly.)* Well I'm sorry but I'm different from all the others. Because I love you. Goodbye.

(She goes towards the door. DRAKE stands frozen, the other two looking at him. Finally, when JULIA is almost out of the door, JAMES speaks.)

JAMES. Well aren't you going to tell her?

(JULIA stops, and turns.)

DRAKE. I, er ....

JULIA. Tell me what?

JAMES. Why he was in such a hurry to get to the bus station.

DRAKE. She'd never believe it.

JAMES. Try her.

DRAKE. She'd lose what little respect she still has for me.

JAMES. Nonsense, she'd welcome you with open arms into the club! Tell her for God's sake. Then she'll understand.

HONEY. *(Stepping forward.)* I'll tell her.

JAMES. *(Fierce.)* Belt up you!

HONEY. *(Taken aback.)* Oh.

JAMES. *(Grabbing her by the arm.)* You've stuck your oar into this little affair quite enough! You and I are going out, and leaving them to swim home on their own.

(He drags her towards the door.)

HONEY. But they might need us.

JAMES. They don't need anybody.

HONEY. Where are you taking me?

JAMES. Back to your place.

HONEY. Oh, goody!

JAMES. Where I'm going to give you what someone should have given you long ago.

HONEY. What's that?

JAMES. The biggest hiding of your life!

HONEY. Oh goody, goody!

(JAMES sighs hopelessly and flings her out through the door.)

JAMES. Get out!

(The door closes. DRAKE and JULIA are left gazing at each other.)

JULIA. Tell me what?

DRAKE. All right Drake, get it over with. It's like this you see, Julia.... I'm not quite what I seem.

JULIA. What you seem?

DRAKE. What you think I am.

JULIA. What are you?

DRAKE. What you are.

JULIA. *(Exasperated.)* What's that for Heaven's sake?

DRAKE. A virgin.

JULIA. A *what*?

DRAKE. A vir .... *(Sighs.)* I've had this conversation so many times.

JULIA. Do you seriously expect me to believe that? After I've sat here all this time, watching them file through like a queue for that bus?

DRAKE. I've missed it every time! That's why I've been making such an idiot of myself.

(Pause. JULIA stares at him, thunderstruck.)

JULIA. *(Her face crumpling.)* Oh my goodness ....

(She is on the verge of tears.)

DRAKE. Not again, Julia, please.

(She flings her arms round him, almost knocking him over.)

JULIA. Kiss me.
DRAKE. Now wait a minute!
JULIA. Kiss me!
DRAKE. You don't understand about me and fate.
JULIA. *Please*, kiss me.
DRAKE. The roof will probably fall in this time.
JULIA. Just one kiss.
DRAKE. Well, it's got to end right there.
JULIA. Right there.
DRAKE. Just one kiss.
JULIA. Just one.
DRAKE. Hold tight. *(Looks heavenwards.)* It's only going to be one kiss, fate.

(They kiss, tentatively at first, then with more passion. In the middle of the embrace MRS. FINNEY emerges from the kitchen with her hat and coat on. She sees them, presses the button in the control panel without pausing, and exits. The bed descends and hits the floor with a thump.)

DRAKE. *(Jumping, startled.)* Ah!

(They look round, see the bed, smile at each other. He picks her up and goes towards the bed as the curtain falls.)

CURTAIN

PROPERTIES

Foam mattress — 3 to 4 inches thick
2 pillows
Pair sheets, pillowcases
Blanket
Bedcover
Suitcase
Shopping bag
Assorted cosmetic bottles
Dressing table stool
Bottle Australian Schnapps (Homemade green concoction)
Champagne bottle — open
Ice bucket with (plastic) ice
Bottle of wine (open)
Whisky bottle — practical
Campari bottle — ditto
Soda siphon
Tumblers
Glasses
Corkscrew
Electric typewriter
Filing tray with miscellaneous stationery
Paper knife
File (Draycott's script)
Typing paper
Fancy notepaper and envelopes
Invoice book
Postage stamps
Large diary
Large envelopes
Photos — fan mail
Tissues
Wastepaper basket
Revolving (typist) chair
Executive case
Bundle fan mail

Newspaper
Miscellaneous dressing for desk
Coffee table
Low candelabra with candles
Ashtray
2 place mats
2 napkins
2 dinner plates
2 side plates
4 knives
4 forks
4 teaspoons (one bent)
2 dessert spoons
Coffee set — Pot and 4 cups, saucers
Milk jug, sugar basin with tongs
2 trays (1 coffee, 1 breakfast)
2 eggcups
Salt and pepper pots
Dressing gown
Bed socks
Sun glasses
Pajama top
Safety razor
Shaving cream

STANDARD SET

STANDARD BED CONSTRUCTION

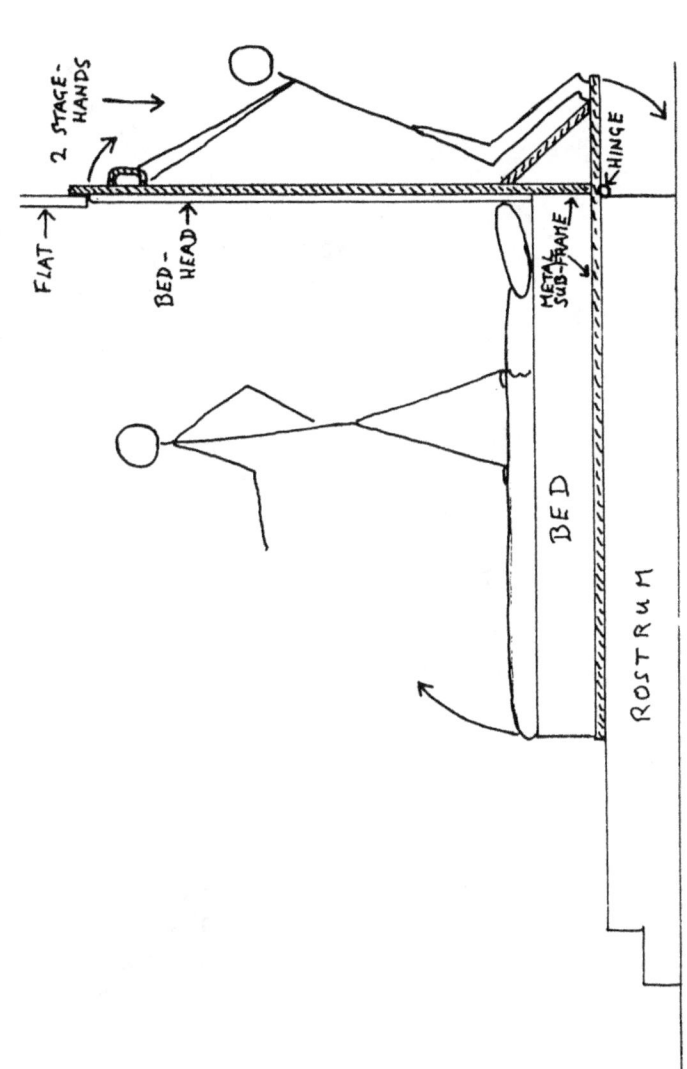

SIMPLIFIED SET

BATH ROOM

BED (TRUCK)

KITCHEN

WARDROBE

FILING CAB

MASKING FLAT

SOFA

FRONT DOOR

BOOKS

SPARE ROOM

FLAP (MIRROR)

DRINKS

FLAP

SIMPLIFIED DESK AND BED SYSTEMS

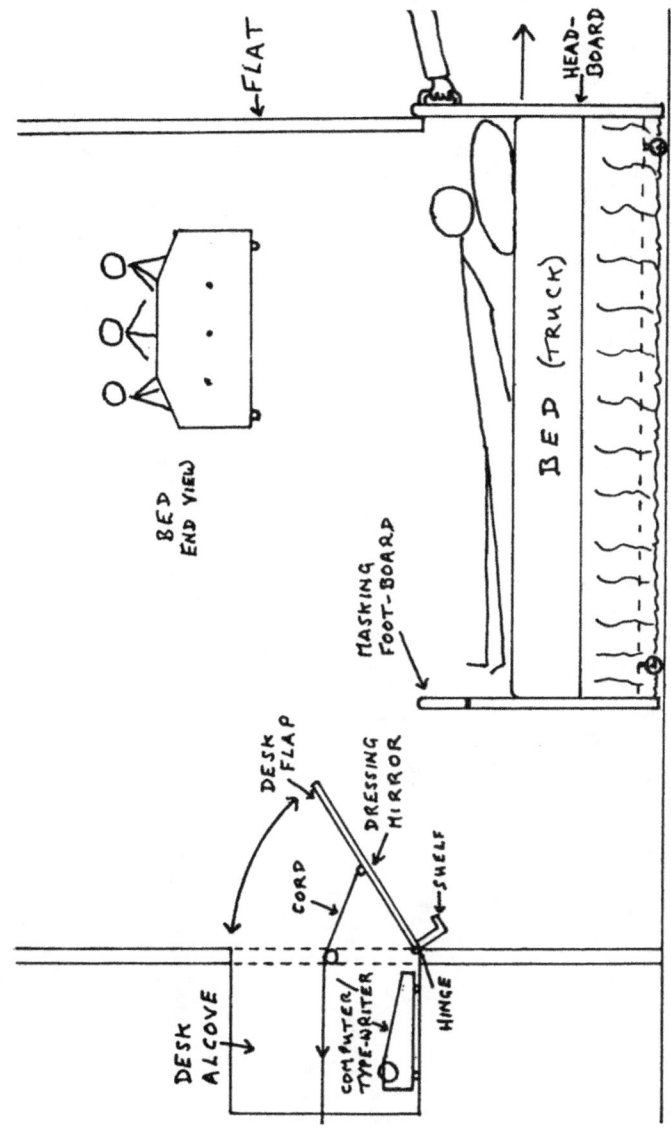

Photo by Reg Wilson